The trouble started when I opened the small door to the broom-closet-sized room that led into the boudoir. The royal purple material, draped so becomingly yesterday, hung slightly askew. Not a big deal. Maybe someone brushed up against it on their way out yesterday. Maybe Jackie had jerked the material in her huff to get away from the likes of me. Who knew? Although I thought I would have seen it before leaving last night.

I had my answer when I walked into the main part of the boudoir. It looked like a freaking cyclone had hit Frederick's of Hollywood. Bras and crotchless panties hung from the previously romantic sconces, like leftovers from a bachelor party. Thigh-high stockings and garters littered the floor. After I did a thorough check, I found every single piece of lingerie, every sexy outfit, every panty or bra, was out of place.

The strangest thing about all this was it appeared all the inventory was there except items over a size fourteen. Weird. Not a single plus-sized bra or panty lay among the ruins of the room. No sexy nightgowns with X-anything on the tags. Nothing. It appeared someone had broken in and made off with all the lingerie for the full-bodied woman.

"What the hell is going on?" I said aloud to the wrecked room. As if on cue, the bell tinkled above the door I'd purposely locked behind me when I came in this morning.

Praise for Misty Simon

"Ms Simon's writing has warmth, her characters seem like real people, and her plotting drew me in as she wove this amazing story of a platonic friendship that's breaking new ground, but not without some doubts on both sides. Emotions run high among this couple and the interfering family and friends who have a vested interest in their happiness, and Misty Simon approaches the emotional element so well that, in the end, I even felt compassionate towards the self-centered man who left his pregnant teenage girlfriend to fend for herself a decade earlier. Put this one on your TO READ list because you won't be disappointed in this cake with added sprinkles."

~*Angie Just Read, The Romance Reviews*

~*~

Poison Ivy

by

Misty Simon

Ivy Morris Mysteries, Book One

Poison Ivy

Cover Art by *Debbie Taylor*

The Wild Rose Press, Inc.
PO Box 708
Adams Basin, NY 14410-0708
Visit us at www.thewildrosepress.com

Publishing History
First Crimson Rose Mainstream Mystery Edition, 2014
Print ISBN 978-1-62830-235-6
Digital ISBN 978-1-62830-236-3

Ivy Morris Mysteries, Book One
Published in the United States of America

Dedication

To Daniel and Noelle, as always.
And to Jan Dunning Button—
the first fan I did not know
who told me how much she loved my books

Prologue

I think sometimes a defining moment in life can hit you out of left field. For example, I had no idea my life would change forever when I opened the mailbox on a bright and sunny September day.

I expected the usual junk mail, and maybe a few bills to add to my growing collection. I found all of that along with a circular for the latest fashions at Sears and a letter from a law office in a place called Kilmarnock, Virginia.

My great aunt lived in Virginia, but I knew she didn't work for an attorney. Come to think of it, I hadn't heard from her in a while.

The thin letter felt heavy in my hand. I barely kept myself from ripping it open as I walked up the driveway. Before I hit the door, I heard my father's booming voice. I could swear it rattled the fronds on the palm tree standing in the dinner-plate-sized front yard.

"Anything good in the mail, Ivy?" my dad yelled from the living room of our old house as I entered the small foyer. "I'm waiting for the Sears catalog."

I was so entranced by the letter and the secrets it might hold, I didn't answer him right away, which earned me yet another eardrum-shaking yell.

"Yes, yes," I said impatiently, and walked toward my father's bellow. I handed him the Sears catalog. At least it would keep him entertained for some time and out of my hair while I read what an attorney from Virginia could want with a girl who'd lived in California all her twenty-four years.

Leaving my father to drool over tools and the latest in flannel, I rushed up the stairs and into my room. My mom had decorated it all in pink shortly before she died, and I hadn't managed to repaint it yet. At ten, the room was beautiful, but fourteen years later it needed an overhaul. I would have loved to paint it a nice taupe, but every time I made some noise about changing the color my dad would get this look of agony on his face and I'd drop the subject. It was a pattern he realized worked well on me, and he wasn't one to change things when they worked, so we were at an impasse. Still, every time I entered the entirely pink domain, I got depressed and wanted out of the room, out of his house. I could keep on dreaming because, as the youngest of four girls and the only one not married, I was stuck here helping him, trying to be a good daughter, when all I really wanted was to break away. Plus, housing costs were so high, there was no way I could afford to live on my own.

From the fuchsia desk on the far wall I picked up a letter opener and made a slit in the envelope. Questions tumbled over one another in my head. What could this be? Could it have something to do with my great-aunt Gertie, whom I hadn't heard from in ages? Why the personal attention? Was it good news or bad news?

Why was I getting worked up over a stupid envelope?

Finally, I wrestled the cheap plastic opener through the heavy paper. For once I didn't snag the letter and cut it in my haste to open the envelope.

Yanking the single tri-folded sheet out, two words jumped out at me like that hot-looking guy my friends hired to burst from my oversized birthday cake last month: your inheritance.

Chapter One

I really appreciate you guys helping with this," I said to the "Bouquet." My three sisters are Daisy, Rose, and Magnolia, so it's a family joke. My guess was our parents ran out of flowers when they reached me. I've often felt blessed I didn't end up as Petunia. Ivy wasn't much better, but I was stuck with it.

They were helping me unpack the few things I'd brought with me to Martha's Point, Virginia, from the pink room of horror. Thankfully, I didn't need much because my newly inherited house came furnished. It turned out the one-page letter was notification of my great-aunt Gertie's passing and my status as her sole heir. It was sad, but she'd been ninety-three and had lived a full life.

"Dad decided not to come because he's sure I'll be back in two weeks, tops." I was bound and determined to prove him wrong.

"I can't believe you're going to run a costume shop, Ivy. You don't know anything about retail," Rose, the voice of reason, said. "You're an administrative assistant, not a proprietress." A small store, The Masked Shoppe, was part of the inheritance, too.

"Good word, Rose," I said. Using big words was a game we'd played for years. "And I will be a proprietress starting Monday. Mr. Winnet, the lawyer, said the store can open then, and I borrowed every book from the library on running a business. I'll beef up my knowledge over the weekend and be ready for Monday. I shop all the time, so surely I can brazen my way through being on the other side of the counter. This will work. I can feel it."

A snort sounded from behind my right shoulder where Maggie was folding towels. "This strikes me as something that takes college classes and experience," Maggie, the teacher, said. "I don't believe you can simply jump in and wing it." Magnolia was the oldest and often the damper on any party.

I made a nasty face at Maggie. "There was a Mrs. Drake at the will reading, and she said she'd help me in any way she could. I got the impression she and Great-Aunt Gertie were tight before Gertie died. Anyway, Mrs. Drake said she used to work in the shop all the time during their busy seasons."

"Well, that's something, at least," Daisy said. "Maybe you won't get into that much trouble with someone helping you. I thank God it's you instead of me." Daisy, the eternal optimist.

A chorus of agreement filled the small bedroom. I knew none of them wanted the store. They were all living their fantasy lives with wonderful husbands and two kids each. In fact, two of them, Daisy and Maggie, had actual white picket fences surrounding their homes.

"I'll be fine, guys. And I want to thank you again for all your help. I feel better knowing you three are firmly in my corner." Okay, so that was a facetious— another good word—statement. But I was out of my father's house and on my own for the first time ever. I'd be damned if I didn't take this opportunity and milk it for everything I could. I wouldn't care if I were selling plastic doll arms and legs as long as I lived on my own. It was a bonus that I would get to sell something as interesting as costumes, from the ordinary to the exotic. Oh, plus I now lived three thousand miles away from the family home.

Unpacking continued, and soon the dinner hour rolled around. We ordered pizza from the only delivery place within twenty miles and settled down with wine in jelly-jar glasses. The heady aroma of pepperoni scented the air. It was time to celebrate my first Friday night in my house.

"So what's your plan for Monday?" Daisy asked, with cheese dripping from the corner of her mouth.

"I thought I'd go in and begin inventory with Mrs. Drake. She said I could familiarize myself with the stock, and she'd help with ordering and ringing up sales. She laughed a lot when talking about what's for sale, which made me a little uneasy. Do you think it's anything risqué or trashy?"

The Bouquet laughed and started naming a variety of costumes they'd like to see me try to sell. The words dominatrix and streetwalker figured prominently in the conversation.

"Promise me you won't wear something beige for your first day," Rose said, and had my back going up.

With my mousy brown hair, fair complexion, and a little bit of extra weight, I thought I looked best in browns. Plus, it had been a way to not draw attention to myself at my last job. Everyone there was about the size of a #2 pencil, and then there was me, the big, fat permanent marker.

"I'll try," I mumbled.

"What?" asked Rose.

Louder, I said, "I'll try. I know I have some colorful things hanging in the armoire Great-Aunt Gertie left. I'll look over the weekend and promise not to wear anything remotely brown. Not even beige. All right?"

"Much better. You need a splash of color." This from Maggie, who had beautiful midnight black hair and looked stunning in anything she put on. She could wear the jewel tones, pastels, black, or stark white. I'm comfortable in brown. But I guess I could step out of my monochromatic wardrobe for one day and try something new. Then again, maybe not. Besides, they wouldn't be here to see what I wore anyway. They'd all leave Martha's Point tomorrow to go back to their perfect lives.

I told them as much, and then wanted to pull the words back because it meant a trip to the closet. They pronounced the lone black skirt in my closet perfect when matched with a purple silk blouse—a Christmas gift from my boss last year. Under penalty of death and the threatened horror of extended stays, they told me to wear that outfit. Being the confrontation wimp that I am, I agreed. The color brown wasn't worth dying over.

As much as I loved my sisters, I was never so happy as the day they all left my dad's house. I finally got first crack at the bathroom each morning. My new house had two bathrooms, but they still managed to push me to the back of the line during their stay with me.

When we'd finally stuffed ourselves silly and drunk enough wine to float a small boat, everyone bunked down in my two available bedrooms to sleep off the effects of our carb overdose.

That Sunday, I spent a lazy morning studying my books and looking at the outfit my sisters had set out for me. The Bouquet had left on a plane out of D.C. the day before without incident, and they'd all called to confirm they arrived home safely. Each took a turn hounding me about not wearing brown tomorrow.

I tried the skirt on three different times throughout the day, and each time my legs still looked like tree stumps coming out from under the knee-length hem. No way was I going to wear something that made me feel like a lumberjack on my first day in my new shop.

I'd wear something brown. But as a concession to the promise I made my three sisters, I'd check out the other businesses in the area for a decent salon. If I happened to find one, I'd see about doing something with my mop of lifeless, dull brown hair.

The air was fresh and turning crisp with the onset of October. Red, gold, and orange leaves hung suspended from the trees standing back from the sidewalk. I hoped the shop would be bustling tomorrow, with Harvest and Halloween parties right around the corner. I couldn't help but compare my new life with my old.

In California it would be another ninety-degree day and few, if any, leaves actually fell from the trees unless the tree was dead. And palm trees never changed color. In the neighborhood where my dad lived—it was no longer my home because I had one to call my own, thank you, Great-Aunt Gertie—city workers had put a ton of the tall, broad-leafed giants along the street when the neighborhood was new. Almost every house had one. But here, they had so many different varieties of trees it was breathtaking.

As I passed a woman raking fallen leaves in her front yard, I added a sturdy rake to my list of things I needed to purchase. It went on the mental list under sweaters and extra jeans. My blood wasn't very thick yet, and it was already cold, which I understood lasted until sometime in March.

The woman, dressed warmly with a bright red sweater, lifted her hand to wave as I walked by. The week I'd been a resident of Martha's Point had taught me that almost everyone here was friendly, unless you were an outsider. I couldn't forget the dead fish I'd found on the hood of my car my first night here. Disgusting, but I'd heard Californians were not wanted in this part of the country. Or any part of the country, for that matter. I had a friend who'd moved to Washington State and changed her license plates in Oregon before the last leg of her trip to avoid the label "damned Californian."

I hoped people would forget where I hailed from as I continued to live here and tried to slip in with the locals. Running The Masked Shoppe ought to help. Besides, it wasn't like anyone was toilet-papering my house or trying to poison me in the local restaurant.

I waved back to the woman and continued down the street. I hadn't spent much time out in the town yet because I'd been busy unpacking. But if I wanted business to come into my shop, I knew I had to give business to other shops. In a town this small, that wasn't a guarantee, but it certainly couldn't hurt.

The street was only two blocks long and you'd probably miss it if you sneezed while driving 35 miles per hour through town. Halfway through the second block I came to a shop named Bella's Best. The name didn't give me a hint as to the nature of the business, but I couldn't miss the large picture with a silhouette of scissors cutting a big head of hair. I'd already walked by all the other shops and this appeared to be the only one to offer women's hairstyling. There was a barber, with one of those rotating candy-striped poles out front, but I wasn't trusting my hair, mousy or not, to someone who probably still used the strop to sharpen his blades.

I won't say this shop with its big-hair advertising looked any more promising, but I walked in anyway. It couldn't hurt. And since it was the only beauty shop, I had no other choice. If I chickened out when I saw the hairdresser (visions of big teased hair the color of autumn maple leaves ran through my mind), I could always get a trim and still have given a local some of my business.

"I'll be right there, hon," I heard a voice yell from the back of the shop as I pushed open the glass-and-chrome door. The vision crowding my head suddenly had a huge beehive hairdo and a bright red mouth furiously working a piece of gum. Someone who wore tight, bright, nubby sweaters and vinyl pants like Dolly Parton in *Steel Magnolias*.

Definitely just the trim.

The saloon-style doors swung open from the back and my vision collapsed and died a grateful death. The voice may have been brassy, but the woman who came through the white doors was as far from the big-hair, tight-sweater group as I could imagine. Flare-legged jeans hugged slender thighs, and narrow feet were encased in those four-inch heels I'd never been able to even think about wearing. Not unless I wanted to walk around with a neck brace for a dozen weeks. She wore a deep blue cowl-necked sweater over the pre-faded jeans and had a beautiful head of mahogany hair with subtle highlights. This woman I could trust with my hair. I felt it in my bones, like when you find a deli or a new flavor of ice cream you can't live without.

"Hi, hon," she said in a drawl that wasn't nearly as thick as I had originally thought. "What can I do for you?"

Suddenly I was a little nervous. Was I ready to let go of the long hair I'd always hidden behind? Would this beautiful woman understand what to do with me—an overweight woman who was seriously hair impaired?

Maybe she sensed my hesitation, because she came over and stood right in front of me. "I'm Bella," she said, and tipped her scissors toward a plaque above the one station in the small shop. "And you're the new girl who's going to run Gertie's shop." It wasn't a question, more like a declaration, so I merely nodded.

"Well then, city girl, we'd better fix you up before your first day tomorrow. You want to impress those old gals who come in and shop for the belly dancer costumes, don't you?"

I pulled my jaw off the floor. "Belly dancing? Seriously?"

She laughed, a musical tinkle, and led me to a chair. "Sure, hon. Didn't anyone tell you the costume shop also doubles as a lingerie store, since we don't have anything else around here? We're not catalog shoppers, either. People don't want *those* kinds of packages going past nosey old Thelma Boden down at the post office."

"Uh, no. No one mentioned the lingerie part. What

kinds of things do people buy over there?" My new friend, Bella, proceeded to tell me exactly what I could expect to supply and how lucky I was to catch her in the shop today since it was usually closed on Sundays. During the entire haircut I kept thinking the Bouquet would laugh their collective asses off if they found out. Dominatrix was mild.

The next day, bright sunlight stabbed through to the backs of my eyelids, and it took me a moment to orient myself. I couldn't be in the pink room because I'd always purposely kept it dark for morning so as not to be blinded by the brilliance of the sun bouncing off the lacquered walls. And I didn't have a boyfriend, so no way was this some dreamy, post-coital wake-up moment.

After a second, the previous week came back in a flash, and I jumped out of bed to greet my first morning as a proprietress. Stumbling, because I was on fast forward, I ran into the bathroom and brushed out my bed head, hoping it would glisten like the hair in the Herbal Essences commercials. I had used a leave-in conditioner, trying to get it all to lie down the way Bella had shown me. The chunky highlights fell nicely around my face and actually made me look thinner. Bonus.

I skipped to the makeup portion of the morning ritual and used the liner pencil without sticking myself in the eye, which was my custom. I also managed to get blush evenly distributed on my cheeks.

Bella had promised to be at the store this morning to give me a support system on my first day. We'd really hit it off and found we had several things in common. She was an avid reader and we both loved

John Cusack movies, so we were well on our way down friendship lane.

My next sprint was to the huge wardrobe my dearly beloved Great-Aunt Gertie had left behind, where I ran a hand over the many outfits hanging in a straight, precise row. Glancing at the black skirt and purple top still lying on the divan in the corner, I decided the highlights were daring enough for now and tugged a tan pantsuit from a hanger. As a concession to the Bouquet, I also pulled a thin purple leather belt from the closet to circle around my waist under the suit jacket.

I dressed in a hurry, threw on a pair of matching flats, and jogged through the entryway. In a heartbeat, I was out the door, with its oval of beveled glass, and on to my future, which, fortunately, was a short walk down the street to the left.

Bless Mr. Winnet's heart, the key to *my* store waited in my mailbox as promised. For a key that had seen twenty years of use, it was shinier than I'd expected. But my enthusiasm for actually having it in my hot little hand overrode any concern lurking in my brain.

I took a moment to enjoy the other small, privately owned shops and round, wooden tubs of flowers on the old sidewalk as I made my way along Main Street. Each store had a very individual look to it. Besides Bella's shop, there was a grocer and a dentist, a vintage clothing store, a used bookstore, and one video store. I might have to get that Netflix thing, because Bella said the video store had only recently started carrying a limited selection of DVDs, and I lived for movies on DVD.

Some stores were renovated old houses and some

were remodeled old buildings. The overall feeling was homey and appealing. I always knew I wasn't a big city girl, and this confirmed it.

A wooden sign painted bright white and deep green announced The Masked Shoppe. I'll admit the name wasn't exactly original. In fact, I'd been giving some thought to changing it to something different, something more, something snappier. But for now, regardless of the lifeless name, it was mine. Really, that was all that mattered. Although, on second thought, the name did have a certain flair, considering I now knew the shop had a dual purpose. Maybe I would keep it.

I felt like a bottle of champagne should be smashed or some other celebratory thing done to commemorate my first time in the store. It had been locked up during the will probate, and the lawyer had asked me not to come into the shop until today. To say it nearly killed me was an understatement. I would have hunted him down like a rabid squirrel if the key hadn't been in the mailbox this morning.

The key slid into the lock with a satisfactory click and turned without hesitation. With a soft drum roll under my breath, I opened the door, ceremoniously taking a bold first step into my new life. And found myself smack in the middle of utter chaos.

Chapter Two

"Holy crap!" I'd been trying to work on the amount of cussing I did. I was now a proprietress and needed to watch my language, unlike when I was a lowly administrative assistant shut in my office all day with no one but my computer screen to hear me snarl dirty words.

I stood for a moment, rooted to the spot. My eyes couldn't figure out where to begin looking. Women and men scurried back and forth between the racks of costumes and what I assumed was the dressing room. I had never been inside the shop before and had been sure I would be alone this morning, the first one to come in. Apparently not.

Mrs. Drake, she of the nice offer to help, spotted me when the doorbell tinkled announcing my entrance. Maybe she'd been blessed with super-bat hearing, because I was standing under the bell and barely heard it. The cacophony of what had to be twenty people, all vying for space in the small store, was nearly deafening.

A smile and a wave of the elderly woman's hand were thrown in my direction. I started to make my way toward the back of the store where the six-foot polished oak service counter was covered with oversized pumpkins and black candles sitting in pools of black silk. Mrs. Drake clapped her hands twice briskly as if she owned the store, and called for everyone's attention. Every head in the store, covered by masks or not, turned her way and silence fell across the room.

"I'd like you all to meet Gertie's great-niece, Ivy, who will be running The Masked Shoppe since our dear Gertie has passed. Now, folks, don't go giving the girl a hard time because she's new." Mrs. Drake cackled, her tiny body vibrating with the sound, though her bubble-like helmet of gray hair did not move an inch.

I felt a little uncomfortable. I mean, this was *my* store, after all. What was she doing making announcements and opening the store before I had a chance to get settled in? I had planned on setting up, getting comfortable, and then opening a few hours late. I'd wanted to go over the books one more time, since I'd only had an hour with them at the attorney's office—pre-ferocious library book studying. Then I thought I'd check out the merchandise to both prepare myself in case I really *did* have to sell dominatrix outfits and to get myself ready for the position as owner, but this woman took it all from me.

Sadly, though, I had never been able to stomach confrontation. So I smiled at all the people who would hopefully put a ton of money in my register, and everyone went back to their decisions on what would be appropriate for this party or that. Mrs. Drake pulled me behind the counter and we talked between customers.

"Dear, I hope you don't mind I opened this morning. With only two weeks before Halloween, I knew we'd be hopping today and wanted to get an early start."

The smile was sweet and the words tumbling from her coral lips were not rude, but there was something about her tone and the "we" thing that made my back go up. Again, I suppressed the snarky words I wanted to throw at her and told myself to be thankful for the assistance. I couldn't have handled this crowd all by myself, but I might have liked the option to try first.

Mrs. Drake—who finally allowed me to call her Kitty after two hours of Mrs. Drake this and Mrs. Drake that—went on to show me how to use the huge, antique register and place special orders. Today was the last day to order anything out of a catalog, because of delivery time. "We like happy customers," she said during a brief lull at the counter. I wasn't stupid—I'll admit to new, but not stupid. Of course we, or rather *I*, wanted happy customers. That was a given.

But I kept the snide comment, begging to be let out, to myself. This inner nasty voice has been popping up more and more as I get older. I don't let it out because of the possible consequences, but lately I've been dreaming of telling just one person to "stuff it." Perhaps I needed to come up with something a little snappier if I ever got the courage to try it.

And I still hadn't revved up the courage to ask Kitty how she opened the store when I was supposed to be the only one with a key, according to the lawyer. I wanted to shake the shit out of my cowardly self and say, "Do it, do it. Ask her." But years of avoiding conflict, added to the fact that the two times in my life I *had* tried wading into an argument it completely backfired on me, now kept me quiet. And mighty disappointed in myself.

After Bella dropped in with muffins and good wishes, I wandered around the shop to acquaint myself with the layout. It wasn't as small as I'd previously thought. Three stalls painted midnight blue, with burgundy velvet curtains, served as the dressing rooms. I followed one of the people I saw go through the only other door in the room and found another surprise.

A closet-sized room sat behind the front room. Two doorways led to and from the claustrophobic space: the one I'd come through and one to another part of the converted house. The small room was decorated with royal purple silk fabric panels hanging from the ceiling and a brocade sofa in complementary colors. Lovely really, but a tad bit big for the space. I opened the other door and entered into a wonderland of silk and lace and ribbons.

Two women, both plump, sat on a chaise lounge, going through little, slinky, see-through black dresses. I knew there was another name for the scrap of material, but other than shameless, I couldn't think of it. Another woman pulled handfuls of crotchless panties from a wicker bin. Okay. This part of the business was not something I'd really thought about since my hair appointment with Bella. It appeared I would have to deal with it now.

"Good afternoon, ladies," I said in my best professional voice, the one I'd been working on all weekend at the recommendation of one of my borrowed books.

There was a twitter that filled the perfumed air. One of the women from the chaise stood up, and I got a really good look at her, along with her big, blond, lacquered hair. She was pear-shaped, with a bit of a stomach, but she had that round, protruding rear end everyone seems to envy these days. She wasn't much older than my twenty-four years, and I hoped maybe I could make another friend in my new town. Two in one week would be great. We could shop and have Girls' Nights. Sip wine at a café—if there was one here, I hadn't checked yet—and tell each other our men troubles. That is, once I had some man trouble to tell about.

I kept that image in my head for the first two minutes as I met Jackie Sturder. I introduced myself and, after finding out her name, offered to help her find the perfect thing out of one of the baskets or the antique armoire.

"I saw this really cute teddy in midnight blue," I said, rummaging around in a white wicker basket hanging from an iron coat rack. I was unfamiliar with the merchandise, but I'd wing it.

I pulled out the teddy in a size I thought was appropriate for her rounded figure and, when I turned around, found she already had another piece draped over her finger. But there was so little material involved in the lace and silk teddy she held, I knew it couldn't be more than a size two.

Jackie, in all her round, curvy glory, was a size two if I could still wear clothes from a children's section. She was closer to a size sixteen, which is still beautiful, but there was no way a two was ever going to fit her.

While I tried to come up with some way to diplomatically get her to buy a size closer to her own, she pulled another small teddy from a drawer in a tall, skinny lingerie chest. Another size two, if I wasn't mistaken, and this one a satin baby doll dress.

Okay, tact was the word of the day. "Perhaps you'd like to look over in this section," I said, still trying to keep customer relations on good terms. I'm all for buying a size smaller to give yourself some incentive, but I'm also honest enough with myself to buy something I had a hope of fitting into on a good day.

"No, thanks," she said. Panties were picked up and discarded or set aside on the top of a short cabinet to her left as she continued to pull from the tall cabinet. I was getting an idea of the way things were set up in this little back room side shop, and she was in the tiny women's section. She wouldn't find anything there that would fit her unless she was looking for underwear to put on her head.

I decided to try again, against my gut instinct, which told me I was not going to get her over in the right area. I wanted happy customers, and I couldn't see Jackie being happy with panties she couldn't wear, especially considering the prices were nothing to sniff at. One of the lines from my very valuable book lessons ran through my head: 'Happy customers are returning customers.' Picking up a pink thong in a sixteen, I walked over to the chest of drawers where she stood. "Maybe these are what you're looking for. They're really pretty and soft to the touch. And, um, sexy." Not my best first pitch as a saleswoman, but I'd tried.

Jackie turned, and her hazel eyes softened as they looked at the frilly pink-and-white lace garment. It was definitely as cute as some of the things manufacturers put out for the slimmer of our species. Her eyes lit up and she rubbed her hands together. I had a sale. Crisis averted and a happy customer all rolled into one. I definitely could do this every day.

I was so proud of myself. I let her take the panties out of my hand and waited to see the expression of joy on her face when she noticed how I worked to please the customer.

Unfortunately it did not go as planned. She unfolded the panties, looked at the size on the distinctive tag, and her eyes went red. I swear fire brimmed in her gaze. She shrieked something in this banshee voice that made it almost impossible for me to distinguish most of her words. I did, however, make out the word "bitch" a couple of times before she stalked out of the lingerie room. She slammed the door with enough force to shake the bells on the revealing belly dancer outfits.

Let me say something here. I had a lot of experience guessing women's sizes from my last job. My boss was a slime ball with a different flavor girl for every month. He frequently asked me to pick something up for whomever he was screwing at the time, and it had to be the right size, as it was always a blouse or some other piece of clothing (to show his sensitive side, and it worked every time, the bastard). So I became adept at knowing the size fours from the size tens, not that there were a lot of size tens. (Hey, I just realized I already had at least one skill honed for this new venture. Yay for me!) Not to mention the fact that I myself was a big, beautiful woman and shopped frequently.

And Jackie was certainly not a two, not even a ten. She was a plus-sized woman, and I found I had plenty of really cute things for the fuller bodied, which surprised and pleased me. I loved lingerie and had had a hard time finding pretty things, not that I'd needed them recently, but that's a different subject.

Jackie, however, was not to be put off from buying a size two. I would have let her, just to have a happy customer, but she had already stomped out.

I raced after her to see if I could salvage the sale. We weren't a large town in any sense of the word, and the grapevine could do horrible things to a small, independent store, according to my *Making a Profit for Dummies* book.

But as I came out from the curtained vestibule, Kitty stopped me in mid-stride by grabbing my arm.

"Leave her be," she said. "She's always in some kind of snit."

Which made me feel better, until she tacked on, "But you may want to watch who you tell what they can buy. It's bad for business to tell the customer they are wrong."

Well, duh. I knew that, and my inner voice shouted in my ears to say something to this woman who really had no right to be in *my* store, much less tell me how to run it. But the coward in me squashed the voice, and I nodded. It was my first day. Maybe I'd say something tomorrow. Or better yet, maybe Kitty wouldn't show up to try and run the store again. At this point I couldn't waste any more time thinking about tomorrow. It was already eleven in the morning, and I'd accomplished very little, other than pissing off a customer and tripping around in a store that was supposed to be mine. Unfortunately, I was feeling more like the employee than the employer.

Chapter Three

The next few hours passed in a blur. I rented out tiger, fairy, and princess costumes to little girls, valiant knights and firefighter costumes to young boys. And to the adult sector: witches and warlocks, adult-sized babies with big diapers and pacifiers. Old ladies with curlers. Pirates waltzed out with maidens. Pumpkins shimmied away with belly dancers (not from the lingerie shop, but the kind that hid at least *some* of the human anatomy while still being sexy). I also did a brisk business from the boudoir, including three leather bustiers and a riding crop, with feathers in black to complement the metallic silver of the handle, that went flying out the door.

Yikes!

But I kept telling myself, "It pays the bills," as I rang up each nasty little purchase. Although when I sold a fat old man a wrestling-style banana hammock in sparkling pink, I felt my gorge rise. You could not pay me enough to see the end result of *that* costume.

As I mentioned before, we weren't a large town, and so there weren't many duplicates, but I did have two separate orders for flapper costumes. Strange, maybe it was a vintage thing. So I rummaged around in the storeroom—another room I'd found at the top of a set of stairs when Kitty pointed—where I finally found the fringed skirts.

There were three of the skirts in the frigid attic. As I looked through more boxes to find the headdresses, one of the skirts kept drawing my eye. It was beautiful, a soft lavender, with sparkles in the fringe that picked up the meager light filtering through the grimy upstairs windows. I imagined myself in the skirt, sashaying my way into the big Harvest Halloween Ball at the Community Center. My invitation had arrived in the mail three days ago, and I'd decided to go. It was good for business, I told myself. Really, though, I wanted to meet some men. I'd been working so hard for the last two weeks—moving, then waiting through the probate, I'd hardly seen anyone, much less any eligible males. Despite Bella's snort when I'd asked about the single male population of Martha's Point, I still hoped some were here and available.

My legs would look really good in the costume. I'd been running around so much lately—as opposed to all the sitting I'd done as a secretary—surely I must have shed a few pounds in two weeks. Plus not having to cook for my dad was an added bonus to the move to my new beloved town. He was a meat-and-potatoes man, and now I could make a salad. And if the salad was all I wanted, I didn't have to suffer through making his dinner anymore. His favorite beef stroganoff was filled with fattening egg noodles that constantly tempted me to taste-test.

It was after eight and the sky was black by the time I trooped down from the attic. I laid out the individual pieces of the flapper ensembles on the counter in the now quiet shop. We, Kitty and I, had closed around six, at her insistence. Why I let her tell me what time to close is still a mystery to me. This was *my* store.

"It's five after six," she'd said with a pointed glance at her imitation leather-banded watch. I could tell time with the best of them, and the large grandfather clock in the far corner had gonged out the hour just minutes ago. I knew what time it was.

"Gertie always closed at precisely six. People set their clocks to the door locking and the lights going off here."

Blah, blah, blah. I ignored her as I continued to polish the counter, hoping she would go away.

Not thirty seconds passed before she started up again. "You know, we won't get any more customers this evening. We've always been done and gone by six. No one will come by after six."

"Kitty, you are more than welcome to go." *And never come back.* "I still have some things I want to do here, but I don't want to keep you past your normal time." Heaven forbid her meatloaf didn't make it to the table when expected.

"Oh, I couldn't do that to you, dear. I wouldn't feel right leaving you here all by yourself. What if you didn't lock up the store properly or couldn't get the day's receipts to balance? Besides, we girls have to stick together. We really should be going. People will think something's wrong if we stay any later. And gracious, someone might actually go so far as to call the police to make sure everything is all right. I bet they'll think a burglary is in progress because the lights are on in here and it's..." She gasped after looking at her watch again. "It's almost six-thirty."

Obnoxious poop. So it was six-thirty. Surely the National Guard was not going to come out because my store was still open. I wanted to tell her to get the hell out, but two things held me back. First, the wuss gene reared its ugly head and I backed down. And second, I didn't know enough about the store yet to take over running it completely without her help. I was in a bind, and you don't bite the hand that rings up the sales. That blasted antique register still baffled me.

After a lot of coaxing, Kitty finally left on her own, without me having to toss her out on her old, flat butt. I tried to subtly insert a little something like, "You're on my turf, playing by my rules," into our brief conversation, but I fumbled. Again.

Once she was gone, I locked the doors and fielded a call from the cops, who were checking to make sure everything was okay and did I know it was after six? Argh. I told them I'd be in the attic until about eight. And that's precisely what I proceeded to do. I did not want some patrol guy to come over to make sure I wasn't stealing from my own store.

I wish someone would put out a catalog filled with things like brass balls and steel backbones. I'd order in a heartbeat.

I jerked myself out of remembering Kitty and the annoyance that seemed to go hand in hand with her. Instead, I concentrated on the pieces and parts of the costumes laid out on the counter in front of me. I set to work on finding any rips or tears—imperfections—in the garments. One fringed top needed mending at the shoulder, but otherwise I was in business. I put the separate pieces into a bag marked with the word CLEANERS and took a soft paintbrush from under the counter to clean the feathers on one of the headpieces.

Anyway, at least now I had the place to myself. And after poking around in the nooks and crannies of

The Masked Shoppe, I fell in love. The bustle and noise had died, and in its place was a quiet Celtic soundtrack playing through the speakers in the rafters. I'd found the coolest old stereo in the boudoir's closet, with a stack of tapes. The system was completely pre-CD. The toe of my shoe tapped out the hypnotic rhythm of the music on the wood flooring.

An okay first day, I thought, and hummed to the music as it whispered across the deserted main room. I'd left the candles burning throughout the day, and they still gave off the welcome smell of apples. Black apple candles. Go figure. Cream-tinted I could see, but Kitty told me a local candle maker would put any dye color on a chosen scented candle for a little extra. Wonder if I paid for those candles? Petty, I know, but I vowed to keep a closer eye on things now that I knew I was not the only one with a key.

And that reminded me about the lack of a return call from my esteemed attorney. Well, I'd worry about it tomorrow. My first day as a proprietress had been worse than I expected. My optimistic side said tomorrow would be better. I snorted at that side, but inwardly still found a little hope that it was right.

Of course, that's never the way things actually work. Instead of a day that could only top the one before, I walked into chaos of a different kind on my second day.

Setting my alarm clock for five, I chose another brown outfit for the day, this one a straight dark chocolate skirt paired with a silk blouse. The skirt brushed my ankles and managed to slim down the overly abundant curves I owned. Tiny leaves in all the colors of autumn floated down from the rounded neck of the silk shirt. I looked good, not that the Bouquet would agree, since it was still brown, but they weren't here.

So back to the chaos. I didn't notice anything at first, because the front of the shop was in perfect order: costumes and props hanging from silver bars attached to the wall, big wardrobe filled with ball gowns and evening formal wear hanging in a straight row, unlit candles ensconced in pretty puddles of black. Perfect, right?

The trouble started when I opened the small door to the broom-closet-sized room that led into the boudoir. The royal purple material, draped so becomingly yesterday, hung slightly askew. Not a big deal. Maybe someone brushed up against it on their way out yesterday. Maybe Jackie had jerked the material in her huff to get away from the likes of me. Who knew? Although I thought I would have seen it before leaving last night.

I had my answer when I walked into the main part of the boudoir. It looked like a freaking cyclone had hit Frederick's of Hollywood. Bras and crotchless panties hung from the previously romantic sconces, like leftovers from a bachelor party. Thigh-high stockings and garters littered the floor. After I did a thorough check, I found every single piece of lingerie, every sexy outfit, every panty or bra, was out of place.

The strangest thing about all this was it appeared all the inventory was there except items over a size fourteen. Weird. Not a single plus-sized bra or panty lay among the ruins of the room. No sexy nightgowns with X-anything on the tags. Nothing. It appeared someone had broken in and made off with all the lingerie for the full-bodied woman.

"What the hell is going on?" I said aloud to the wrecked room. As if on cue, the bell tinkled above the door I'd purposely locked behind me when I came in.

Chapter Four

I cowered. I couldn't help it. I heard the jingle of the bell and ran behind one of the sheer curtains in the lingerie room, cringing like a kicked dog. I was alone, freaked that my store was broken into and all the larger-sized lingerie was gone.

Well, not alone anymore, but I had been.

My brain finally kicked in when I heard Kitty's strident voice singing some tune from the fifties. So she *did* have her own key and felt confident enough to use it without asking me first. We'd see about that.

I walked out of the back room as if I were on a mission. And I was. I was going to get that key and put Miss Kitty in her place while doing it.

The diminutive lady had dressed in black polyester slacks and a bright orange cardigan the color of that breakfast drink my mom used to make me down by the gallon. Kitty was humming now and I didn't want to scare her, so I cleared my throat and waited for her to turn around.

Jumping a little—which pleased me, although I had just thought about the evils of scaring her—Kitty whirled around and put her hand to her heaving breast. Okay, I admit to feeling a little vindictive at this point. She was in *my* store, uninvited, and hopefully her imbalance would give me the upper hand in the confrontation ahead.

Was I up for it? Again, we'd see about that.

"Kitty," I said, all sunshine and light. "What a surprise. You didn't say you'd be in this morning." I'd delivered the first line and waited for her response. I wasn't going to say another thing until she did. Let her sweat, I thought. She probably had no idea I was upset about her trying to take over the store. I'd bet she was one of those women who saw herself as "helping." And I'd be the bitch who kicked her out. Well, not kicked her out, because I still needed her. Put her in her place. Maybe later I'd go out and kick a poodle.

"Well, Ivy, good morning. I didn't think anyone else was here. I thought I'd come in and get things going for you so you didn't have so much to do. We could have another rush like yesterday, and I didn't want you to be behind."

How thoughtful, I mused. But I wasn't falling for it again. The nice-lady act with the veiled barbs was not going to float this time.

"I certainly appreciate your concern, Kitty. But I've been here for about an hour, and I think you'll find everything in order." Please, God. "I'm taking my responsibilities to the store very seriously. You don't have to worry about coming in early to help anymore. If you'd like to stay on for our peak season, I'd appreciate that, too, but I think normal business hours are fine from now on. In fact, why don't you go ahead and give me your key, so I don't scare you like I did this morning. I can handle opening the shop." I put my hand out for the key and watched as she took her sweet time retrieving it from her purse.

"Really, Ivy. I thought you'd be glad for the help with opening."

Jeez, she was going to drag this out. I thought I'd done pretty good on putting my foot down and didn't want to explain myself to her. I shouldn't have to, and I didn't want to make enemies in my new hometown. So I throttled back my agitation and said, "As I said, I do appreciate your help, and"—I almost choked on the next words—"I would love for you to continue to help, but I think it is a good idea for me to have all the keys for the store. I don't want any confusion over who's doing what, where." Like stealing all the lingerie. Something flickered in Kitty's eyes when I said *all* the keys. Could she have made another one? I didn't know, but I'd have to figure out a way to discover the truth.

She seemed to accept my decision. Finally. This backbone stuff was a lot of work. Of course we had to go through the whole thing of working the key off her enormous key ring, and then the hesitation before she put it in my hand. She started to protest again. I saw the words on the tip of her tongue and cut her off before she could utter the first syllable.

Grabbing the key out of her wrinkled hand, I said, "Thanks, I think this will work out far better." Then I thanked my lucky stars when the bell tinkled again. This time a new customer came in, and I looked forward to another busy day. One in which I'd have to order a bunch of new plus-sized lingerie to replace what was gone and figure out who in their right mind would only take the bigger stuff and leave all the other clothes and costumes, not to mention the cash register. Plus, I didn't want to broadcast the news of the robbery. What if Kitty had taken it all? What if Jackie had come back to exact revenge after our little That Teddy Won't Fit Over Your Thigh tussle?

But all of that took a back seat because the bell tinkled three more times, and my little shop was off and running for the day.

The next few days whipped by in a flurry of cats and bats and vampires, oh my! Everyone in town had passed through my door, and I was happy each night when I counted the till. Kitty didn't show up unannounced again, and we were only a little over a week from the annual Harvest Costume Ball. For the first time in a long time I felt good about damn near everything in my life. It was scary; I kept waiting for the other shoe to drop.

I still worried about the missing lingerie, but the woman at Sass and Lace overnighted some new things and I was able to re-stock the back room without alerting anyone to the theft. I knew I should go to the police, but I wanted to sit on things for a few days before I reported anything. I mean, what would I say? Some larger woman may have made off with my undies? Merchandise was stolen from my store and, by the way, I think you can rule out anyone who isn't at least a size 14? I don't know that they would take me seriously. *I* probably wouldn't take me seriously.

Besides, I'd read a bookshelf full of mysteries. I bet I could figure this one out myself, with my first suspect being Jackie. Maybe she'd stolen the lingerie so she wouldn't have to admit a size two really wouldn't fit her left thigh.

I got my chance the following Thursday. Jackie came in to pick up a kitten costume in a size Large (no argument from me), and I cornered her before she had a chance to walk back to the boudoir.

"That costume will look great on you," I said with

my professional smile on my face. No harm in buttering up the suspect before grilling her like a cheese sandwich.

I got a nod and a cross between a snort and a throat clearing in return. Okay, time to try again. "How are things going with Charlie?" I asked. I'd pumped Kitty for information on Jackie earlier, so I had some conversation openers. Of course I didn't tell her what I needed it for, and, voila, found out Jackie was dating Kitty's son, Charlie. No wonder I got a sense Kitty didn't like Jackie that first day. Nothing like a mama bear protecting her thirty-five-year-old cub from the unworthy paws of the replacement for his affections.

Jackie's whole body went stiff as a board, and I was puzzled. I didn't come out and say "Can you please return my stock" or anything, so why go statue on me? Maybe there were problems in paradise.

But then a smile came across her face and she seemed to relax. It was a nice smile, but I could see a hint of smugness there. I was confusing myself with all these mixed messages, so I gave up the over-analyzing. I'd try later when I wasn't being knocked off my feet with the overpowering reek of too much of Elizabeth Arden's *Red*.

"Charlie's great." Jackie brushed her blond hair over a rounded shoulder. "Thanks for asking. Hey, I wanted to apologize for the other day."

Wow. I hadn't seen that one coming. Now I was the statue. For about two seconds. "Um...thanks." So did I have to apologize here, too? No way. I had nothing to apologize for. I'd thought some unkind things about her since the Back Room Debacle, but everything I'd said to her at the time was true. Then again, I could have been nicer, and maybe I should apologize for that. She was a customer, and I wanted happy customers.

She saved me from further self-torment by waving her hand as she walked away from me. Well, that went better than I'd expected. Or did it? I pondered the smug smile as I went about the rest of my day. Did it mean she knew something about the missing lingerie, or was I reading too much into nothing? Maybe her smiles were always smirky? Maybe I'd have to check out the next person on my short list of suspects.

I locked up the store and went home to my clawfoot tub for a long soak. Bella was taking me out tonight to see the town, and she had told me to dress casual. That didn't mean I couldn't look damn good in casual. After all, I still hadn't seen any really eligible men yet, and if I happened upon the one that (hopefully) existed in this town, I wanted to be prepared. Not desperate for the earth to swallow me whole because I hadn't put on enough deodorant or my hair looked like I'd stuck my finger in an electric socket.

So I searched through my closet—and shuddered because Bella had been right about my limited wardrobe. I had brown skirts and khaki pants, copper shirts and umber blouses, cocoa tanks, and even a pair of sepia jeans.

It occurred to me, standing amidst yards and yards of brown garments, that perhaps I had taken the one compliment given to me at my old job a little too seriously. I'd worn a chocolate-hued pantsuit with a light beige blouse and my boss, for the first time in three years, had said I looked nice. Knocked me for a loop, and I guess it shut down the rest of my color sense.

Damn. What was I going to do now? Obviously, the only sane thing I could think of—I called Bella.

"Help!"

"Ah, let me guess," she said, voice smug over the line. "You looked through your closet and can't find a single blessed thing in any color other than brown."

"You're psychic now, too?" That could certainly be a big help with my lingerie thief.

"No," she said. "I've seen you over the last two weeks, and every piece of clothing you've worn has been, in one shape or form, brown. The jeans you wore last week blew me out of the water because they were actually blue. But that's been it as far as diversity in color."

"I know," I wailed. No shame in wailing when it's over clothes. Well, clothes and shoes. I wouldn't wail over underwear that was brown. That thought caught me off guard and I pawed through my chest of drawers, only to discover bras and panties of every cut and material, but all in shades of brown. Shit. Well at least no one would see my undies tonight. Tomorrow I'd raid the lingerie room at work, assuming the thief didn't come back. He or she had taken everything last week, including my size—which we'll call ten because I'm having a Jackie day.

"Hey, no whining. Look, we can fix this. Come over right now and we'll find something for you."

"Yeah, right. As if you have anything that would fit me." I tried hard for the no whining, but I was pretty sure I did not hit my mark.

"I said, no whining." Nope, guess I didn't. "Just get

over here. ASAP."

So, after applying my makeup with an eye toward covering my enormous pores (why couldn't I have silky smooth skin to counterbalance the weight?), I jumped into my sand-colored Hyundai Santa Fe—color police help me!—and zipped the three blocks to Bella's cottage.

The little house was painted a bright, sunny yellow, and a bold red coated the front door. It sat nestled in a flood of color, flowers spilling from baskets and planters, from gardens and windowboxes. Thank God I hadn't planted anything at Great Aunt Gertie's house yet. What kinds of flowers are brown and still alive?

Even her house shouted confidence, I thought as I walked up the cobblestone pathway. Fountains with open-mouthed fish and fairies pouring water from chalices stood in the emerald green of the lawn.

I knocked, and before my fist landed back at my side, the door whipped open and Bella dragged me over the threshold into a wonderland of jewel tones and light wood. She shoved me in front of her as we walked down a short hallway, so I didn't get a chance to admire any of the blur of colors.

"So much for hello," I said.

"No time. Strip and start trying on the things I put on the bed."

Hoo-kay. But when I turned to see the clothes strewn across the lavender comforter, I gasped.

"These are beautiful." I fondled one silk blouse in electric blue paired with a long slim black skirt.

"Less talking, more trying."

She didn't have to tell me twice, although there was no way I was going to change in front of her and her little compact body. In her rose-and-cream bathroom, I shrugged out of my beige shirt and brown slacks and pulled on the black skirt. The silk lining under the wool slid up the length of my legs and I buttoned the side, turning toward the mirror. It's always a test for me to see if slacks or skirts look all right by themselves without the long shirt I usually drape on.

And the skirt fit like a dream. No extra flesh hanging over the top. No smushing of my slightly rounded stomach to ruin the lines of the garment. I seriously contemplated never taking it off.

Then came the blouse. I'll admit here that I've never worn bright colors because I always thought they'd drain me of what little color I possessed. I didn't have one of those peaches-and-cream complexions. I wasn't tanned, even though I had lived in California for all my twenty-four years. If I had to pick a color to describe myself, it would have been wheat and washed out, certainly not glowing. But when I put that unlikely electric-blue blouse on, I knew I lit up like a saloon sign on a Friday night. Bella told me as much after I stumbled out of the bathroom in a haze of excitement. Oh, and my own eyes confirmed it.

"Now, that is what I'm talking about," Bella said, a triumphant smile on her vivid face. "You look great. That color brings out the blue of your eyes and makes your hair shine." She made a motion for me to turn all the way around, and I did. "Yes. Definitely. You should burn all your brown clothes."

"Absolutely not." I liked the new colors, but I wasn't willing to abandon brown altogether. The Masked Shoppe wasn't bringing enough money into my checking account to allow a new closet full of clothes.

Plus, I'd set up Kitty's son Charlie with the plum job of putting a fountain in the main room. I'd looked and looked for someone else, but the supply of good handymen was way down in this town.

"Absolutely, yes. You can start by burning this brown blouse and then taking the rest of the clothes on the bed home. Right after my divorce, I gained twenty pounds from the stress, but I wasn't going to dress like it. So I bought all these clothes with my ex's credit card and left him with the bill." A feral grin spread over Bella's painted lips and I smiled with her.

"Well in that case, I guess I could be ready for a change. Wouldn't want a whole payback shopping spree to go to waste. Should we make it like a celebration?"

"Yes." Bella threw another pair of pants on the bed, these in a bright, almost luminescent green. I didn't know if I'd ever be able to actually walk outside in them, but it would be fun to open my closet and know they were there.

"It will have to wait, though," she said as she emerged from the walk-in closet with a pair of black stiletto heels. "We need to get you ready for tonight. Your liberation from brown can be this weekend, but your liberation from celibacy can be this evening."

How did she know I'd been without male companionship of the sweaty kind for a couple of years? Maybe it showed on my face or in my choice of clothes. Either way, I hoped she was right and the drought would be over soon. I stepped into the stilettos, praying I wouldn't break my neck when I fell into the arms of a handsome stranger.

Chapter Five

We walked into the Rusty Pelican and my first thought was, Club? This was what they considered a club around here? My God, this place was a cross between a dive and a honky-tonk.

L.A. had clubs, and they looked nothing like this. But I decided to think of it as a bar in my attempt to be a part of the culture of my fellow Martha Pointers, as I'd heard locals refer to themselves. Being from Martha's Point and all. Classy, I know.

The motif was distinctly seafaring, with heavy rope nets holding plastic crabs and seagulls. The tables were high, like you'd find in a club, but there the resemblance ended. On top of a ship's wooden steering wheel, turned on its side, similar to the one Captain Jack manned in *Pirates of the Caribbean*, sat a round of glass. The table was certainly unique, and the grips of the wheel stuck out a couple of inches past the edge of the tinted glass. Please, please don't let me start out the night by impaling myself on one of them, I thought.

Smoke and dim lighting obscured the other patrons. Used to California laws, I had completely forgotten Virginia didn't embrace the no-smoking-indoors thing. This would be a pleasant night, complete with my mascara running from my smoke-sensitive eyes. Yay.

I followed Bella to our very own round wheel table

in the corner and thanked my lucky stars there was a vent directly over my head. Maybe this wouldn't be so bad.

Ten minutes later, I knew my stars were out of whack. The vent pulled the smoke our way and yes, indeed, my eyes were starting to stream. We'd been approached by a couple of guys, but Bella shooed them away. After they moved off, she'd lean over to tell me their flaws, which ranged from married to inbred.

But then the door swung open and it was like one of those kooky movie moments. A man walked through the front door and stood silhouetted in the muted light of the bar. He was tall and, from my vantage point in my very attractive captain's chair (no lie, I swear), he looked good. Of course, throughout the evening I'd met and been wrong about Will, the fisherman with the wandering eye, and Chuck, the jobless drifter—and not in a sexy, Brad Pitt in *Thelma and Louise* way. Bella leaned over again and I prepared myself for the inevitable, "He's not right for you. He has slimy hands, syphilis, a wife, etc."

So I was shocked when she said, "Now this is a man who is worth knowing."

What? A man worth knowing? As in biblically? Or because he could build me an ad campaign that would bring in more customers? So I asked. No sense being in the dark if I had a line to the flashlight. "He doesn't have some strange disease or defect I should watch for?"

"No," she yelled in my ear to be heard over the awful '80s cover band wailing out Van Halen, and I waited for the rest. "He's really sweet and kind. I think you guys will hit it off great."

What? again. Hit it off great? So why hadn't she mentioned this fine example of maleness prior to now? Bella had made it a point to let me know I'd have to go outside our small town to find anyone even remotely interesting. So what bushel had she been hiding this one under? And why?

The why wasn't answered immediately, but the bushel thing became clear after she told me where he worked. "He's the food critic for the *Martha Herald*, our local weekly paper. The paper sucks, because it's pretty much all gossip and how to sauce your apples, but he's pretty witty at spotlighting the local restaurants."

So what took up all his time if he only did reviews of local places to eat? I mean, that can't take all day, every day. Can it? Bella's clairvoyance reared its head again, and it was spooky.

"It doesn't take up all his time. He's also doing some online correspondence course work for his private investigator license."

"Online? Seriously? To be a private investigator?" I yelled. And of course, because my stars were in whacked mode, *he* walked up to the table at the precise moment the music stopped and everyone in the place heard me. I fidgeted in the chair, then leaned forward to whisper my embarrassment to Bella. As my stiletto-shod foot slipped off the circular rail, I lost my balance and fell face first into a solid wall of muscle.

Swallow me whole, floor. Open up and take me away. Or was that Calgon?

"Yes, online," a voice as smooth as scotch said right next to my ear. So not only did he have the silhouette thing going for him, but the voice was a potential puddle factor.

Bella, bless her smug heart, jumped right in and made the introductions. Which in no way detracted from my embarrassment like everyone always thinks a change of subject will. Oh no, it just hastened the creeping blush making its way from my chest to my ears. I tried to find the positive here and came up with, "At least it's dark and smoky." Lame, but I so did not need anything else to be mortified about.

"Ben, this is Ivy Morris. Ivy, Ben Fallon." On the first pass, I thought she'd said Fallen. That wouldn't have been far off the mark in features, now that I could see him up close. Too close for a first encounter. Could he see my gigantic pores I'd tried so hard to hide with foundation?

He set me back on my chair like I weighed nothing, and let me tell you, that is some kind of feat. My insides went all fluttery, as though I'd harvested a bunch of cocooned caterpillars.

I finally got a really good look at all of him, and he was the embodiment of my every wish of a fallen angel. Dark hair brushed the collar of his chocolate (see, not a bad color, at least not on him) leather jacket. Moss-green eyes stared into mine, hard cheekbones and a square jaw boxed in a set of lips that should have been illegal—perfect, full lips I wanted to bite. "Uh, hi, Ben."

Brilliant.

Jeez, get it together, Ivy. I didn't even know this guy and already I was wanting to nibble at him? And sounding stupid while I dreamed up my fantasy? Celibacy was obviously not for me when faced with broad shoulders and—if he'd just walk away, I'd put money on it—a fine ass.

In the interest of testing out my theory, I drained my fruity drink and said, "Ben, would you mind terribly getting me another drink?" Which would have been smooth if we weren't sitting two feet from the bar, but he seemed to take the hint. Falling for my lame attempt at a Southern twist on my words, he walked away. Yes, yes, yes! I seriously would have won that butt bet.

"Christ on a crutch, Bella. I thought you said no eligible men. And thanks so much for letting me yell as he walked up." My inner voice sure was coming out more often. Three weeks ago, I would have smiled demurely and let the words run through my head. Or I would have come up with them three hours later and wished I'd said them at the right time. Now I seemed to be blurting out whatever came to mind. I would need to seriously consider investing in a filter between my brain and my mouth. There was certainly something to be said for a little tact.

Bella had the nerve to laugh, a big guffaw, and pat me on the hand. I wanted to smack her, but fortunately the link between my brain and physical abuse had a strong filter of its own.

"Calm down," she said. "From the way he was looking at you, you probably could have yelled out what kind of underwear he wears and he still would have gone to fetch you a new drink."

"Somehow I doubt Ben would appreciate a public discussion of whether he wears boxers or briefs." The music was still loud, so I felt safe in my response. Except my stomach did a slow dive and shivers danced down my back when "Boxers" was whispered into my ear. *Hello, God, anytime now, floor opening up, earthquake, anything?*

Of course, none of those things happened and I had to wait while the blush I was positive flared on my face went from a burning red down to a faint tingle. I used the time to shoot daggers at a smiling Bella.

Ben placed our drinks on the glass table and pulled up a captain's chair for himself, not a self-conscious bone in his body. He plopped into the chair in a decidedly masculine sprawl and threw me a wicked grin.

Sheesh, was it suddenly very hot in here for a late autumn night?

"So, Ivy, Bella tells me you're running The Masked Shoppe now." The '80s cover band was taking a welcome break from their ear-splitting renditions of "White Snake," "Damn Yankees" and "G-N-R," so we could actually talk at an almost normal level. Well, a little louder than normal in order to compete with the other patrons, because it seemed like the whole town was here.

"Gertie was my great-aunt," I said. Duh. I mean, everyone must know that little tidbit in a place the size of Martha's Point. I cleared my throat and plunged on. "I love this town. I'm sorry that Gertie passed, but it got me out of my dad's house." Oh. My. God. I was an idiot. I did a little half-smile and waited for Ben to pick up his glass and move to another table to get as far away as possible from the lunatic who didn't get out of the house unless someone died. Add on the embarrassing fact that it was my dad's house and Ben should be running like a bat out of my hell.

But, surprisingly, he stayed and started telling Bella and me funny stories about the food critic business and local gossip he picked up around the newspaper.

I tried my hardest not to snort at any time and had nearly made it through the first half an hour without embarrassing myself when he said, "So this guy comes in to the paper and wants to place an ad. Not my department, but I was the only one there on that Saturday. So I gave him the template to fill in and waited while he labored over the four lines allowed. He hands the sheet back to me when he's done and I skim over it to look for any misspellings when the words 'crotch' and 'humping' jump out at me. I take a closer look, because I wasn't really reading it for content." Ben took a pull on his beer, then continued, "It turns out this guy found a dog on the side of the road and other than the fact that it's a mutt, the guy put in distinguishing characteristics such as the dog likes to stick his nose in every female crotch he comes in contact with and likes humping hedges."

And I lost it. Just like that, I started laughing so hard I was snorting and then the snorting turned to almost gagging, which is always attractive.

Bella, friend that she was, whacked me a solid one on the back, and I nearly fell off my chair again. This time straight into Ben's lap. Without thinking, I put my hand out to stop my forward momentum and ended up with my fingers grasping a purely male characteristic.

"Holy hell," I said in the silence following my fall. Every eye in the place was on me. Even the bartender had stopped wiping the long, curved bar to look my way. It was the final straw. I awkwardly lurched to my feet and, despite three of the fruity drinks floating in my system and clouding my brain, hightailed it to the ladies' room.

The fake wood door banged shut behind me and I was surrounded by that special scent of public restrooms everywhere—a mix of disinfectant and the last patron who sat on the toilet.

How was I going to face Ben again? He was a lot of things I always told myself I would look for in a guy if I ever met any outside of my old job. Cute, sexy, intelligent, with a hell of a sense of humor. Why, oh, why, did I have to touch his doodads on the first meeting? I totally copped a feel, and while I was embarrassed about the impromptu groping, let me tell you, girls, that had been some serious package to get my hand on. Faint-worthy, even, if I hadn't been so busy turning bright red.

With another loud bang of the door against cheap fabricated wood paneling, Bella came steamrolling into the bathroom and stood before me with her hands on her hips. "You've been gone for ten minutes," she said. "That's long enough. Ben is not annoyed or turned off by your mistake." I'm telling you, she was clairvoyant. I didn't care what she said anymore. "He's out there waiting for you."

"Yeah, waiting for me to come out and make a bigger fool of myself," I said. "You do realize that I am three for three." I ticked items off on my fingers. "I insulted his education, speculated on his underwear choices, and almost made my own in-depth study of the latter right through his pants. What reason, other than further embarrassment, could he possibly have for waiting?" I was close to tears. A burning started in the back of my throat, and my eyes felt itchy. Never a good sign, because I was so not one of those pretty criers who dab at their glistening eyes with a fine handkerchief. I was the puffy-eyes type, snot-honking into plain tissues.

So now I had a choice to make. I could go out and face Ben and see if Bella was reading all the signs right, or I could find an exit that didn't pass by our table and hope to never see the magnificent Ben ever again in my natural life. The Pre-Inheritance Ivy would have run like the devil was on her ass. But the new Ivy... Well, I took stock of myself, swiped a quick hand (not the one that had landed in Ben's crotch—I thought I'd wait to wash it, or maybe I'd never wash it again) over my chunky highlights and told myself I really had nothing to lose. What was the worst that could happen? He could laugh at me and tell me I was a joke. Well, that would be his loss. And since I'd already copped a feel, I was all the more interested in pursuing something that would get me skin to skin with him, without the denim in between.

Chapter Six

In the end, I decided not to hide in the bathroom like a virgin on prom night and instead went back to the table, but I took my time getting there. Would things be weird now that I'd acted like a freak?

"Hi," I said, and jumped back into my captain's chair. I figured I'd try to act like nothing had happened and see how that went over. I didn't think I'd be able to get too cozy with Ben again, but I at least wanted to be able to feel comfortable looking him in the eye if I saw him around town.

Bella and Ben both said "Hi" at the same time, then looked at each other and started laughing. I felt curiously left out of the loop.

"So, Ben, how long have you been working for Martha Point's only paper?" Not a great question, but if I wanted to eventually get a more intimate hold on him, as in sans clothing, I really needed to know more about him. My body might want him, but my mind needed to want him, too, or it would never work. I'd had one one-night stand when I was twenty, and even four years later it was still enough to convince me never to participate in something like that ever again.

"It's been what, like seven years now, right, Bella?"

Again I felt left out and then reminded myself everyone who lived in Martha's Point had been rooted here for a lot of years, if not their whole lives. I'd never have the kinds of relationships they had. Well, maybe when I was sixty and still here, but not any time soon. I was the new girl, and probably would be for the next ten or eleven years.

"Yeah, I think you were twenty when you started. But don't forget, you also had a paper route, so you have to add a couple more years. I can't believe they let you throw papers for that long." She paused and looked at me for the first time since she'd said hi. "He had a mean arm, but the paper just never made it to the front porch. He'd throw the right distance but in the wrong direction. My mom wanted to tan his hide for ruining her perennials every year." She smiled at Ben, and I got a weird feeling in my stomach.

Oh, God, was I encroaching on her territory? She had asked me to come with her tonight, and told me Ben was someone worth knowing, but Bella hadn't come right out and said he was available. How could I ask without making a fool of myself? And then it came to me. "So you two have known each other for a long time?"

"Oh, yeah," Ben said. "Forever. We went to kindergarten together, and Bella was my first kiss." He smiled fondly at Bella, and I was torn between choking my new friend and puking because I'd had my eye (and my hand. Oh. My. God.) on someone who was already taken. That was a big huge Absolutely Not in my book on how to run my life. I was back to wanting the floor to open up and take me.

Bella hit his upper arm playfully. "You are an idiot, Ben. That was in second grade, and I haven't let you touch me since." She laughed, Ben laughed, and finally

I could laugh without gagging.

"And have you kissed every other girl in town, too?" I asked the question before the inner tact-ometer could filter. Shit!

But Ben didn't even miss a beat. "Only the pretty ones."

Well, then, I had no chance in hell of finding out if those lips were as firm as they looked.

Ben leaned forward. "So, Ivy, you want a kiss?"

My fallen angel smiled as he waited for my answer. I could tell he thought he already knew what it would be, and I wanted so badly to show him I wasn't some naïve girl who could fall so easily under his charms. Or under him, period, just yet, though that thought did make my innards tingle. But it might make him take notice if I was a little aloof. "Hmmmm. Well, I don't know. I mean, who knows where else those lips have been? And we haven't even danced yet. I don't think you've done anything to earn one of my kisses."

"Then we'll have to take care of that right now." He stood up and made a move to grab my hand.

"Actually, Ben, as nice as that sounds, I need to get going. How about some other time?" I'd looked at my watch and noticed it was getting late. I wanted to get home early tonight because tomorrow was the day before the Ball and I had a bunch of people scheduled to pick up their rentals for the big evening. I'd probably have quite a few last-minute items purchased, too. It was going to be a busy day, and I needed to be fresh to face it.

I wasn't really trying to be coy, but I think it came off that way, because Bella winked at me, and Ben looked like he'd been sucker-punched for about a second before he recovered.

"I'll hold you to that, Ivy. Save me a dance on Saturday, and we'll see if I can't earn a kiss. And maybe more." Picking up his beer, he walked away backward, waving goodbye. Then he turned around and I was treated to a view I was coming to love.

"That certainly got his attention, Ivy," Bella said with approval and a nudge to my arm. "I don't know that anyone has ever played hard-to-get with Ben. This ought to be interesting."

Interesting? Maybe, but who was that girl flirting with Ben and coming up with lines like "You haven't earned a kiss"? I was so not the old Ivy I used to be. But was I really ready to take on this new persona? I could only hope.

The next day I went home after the busy day I'd anticipated and spent hours tossing and turning until I finally fell asleep, only to be visited by some pretty hot dreams of Ben in nothing but a pair of socks—green striped ones. I don't know what it meant, but it was some view. Sigh.

Those dreams kept me entertained through another long day of battling with the antique cash register and dealing with Kitty and a number of frantic customers who needed that one last thing to make their outfits complete. Now there were only three hours left before the Harvest Ball started, and I was still trying to figure out what to do with my hair. Bella had given me this great new cut and worked some serious magic so that layers fell around my face, softening it. My highlights hadn't grown noticeable roots yet, and although the new look was a good one for me, I didn't know how to fix it. I should have waited until after the Ball. Note to self: don't change hair right before an important function unless you are really good with hair. Which I wasn't, and so my dilemma.

I'd already changed into my flapper costume. My legs actually looked fabulous in the fishnet stockings, and I'd solved the whole fear-of-flab-on-the-arms thing by making a great web shawl.

Tonight promised to be a blast. Only Bella knew what costume I'd chosen, and I was excited to show it off at the Ball. I'd never looked this good before. The mask I'd found was perfect for the outfit—feathers and sequins captured the light and reflected it back from the black mask. It covered my eyes, and something about the way it was cut made my cheekbones look sharper. Very flattering.

All in all, I was extremely optimistic about tonight. Anyone who hadn't made it to my shop within the last two weeks would get an eyeful of what I could do with a few simple pieces, and my beauty would dazzle the rest.

Yeah, I know, that was going a little far, but tonight was all about the possibilities. I'd talked Ben into a Zorro costume that showed off his very fine rear end to the best advantage. Maybe he'd carry me away on his stallion before the night was through. That thought alone was worth a good fifteen-minute trip to fantasyland, but we'd been so busy today, it would have to wait until I could get my hands on the real thing.

I'd shaved my legs and made sure to pay special attention to my knees. I had issues with my knees. I never had a problem shaving any other part of my body to perfection, but for some unknown reason the knees thwarted me every time. But not today. Today I used wax and Nair and a pair of tweezers with a magnifying glass. I was so not taking chances, especially with these very airy stockings.

The Ball was scheduled to start at seven at the Old Barn, which Bella told me really was a barn in another life and used to house horses and pigs. Fortunately, that was about a hundred years earlier, and she assured me the smell had long ago dissipated. Some enterprising farmer had decided to ditch the whole livestock thing and make an elegant hall available to the town in the early 1920s—hence the flapper costume. Sometimes I was way too clever.

I spotted a wig left out on the counter and walked over to put it back on its fake head just as the bell over the door tinkled. I was seriously considering taking the bell down and getting one of those electronic chime things. But I was afraid the missing bell would create a catastrophe. Take the fountain Kitty's son was putting up on the far wall. He was doing an incredible job on it, and I'd taken a liking to him despite his awful taste in girlfriends. And his mother? Well, you can't pick your parents.

Unfortunately, you would think I'd razed the store and started a porn theater the way people were gawking at the wall where my pretty mermaid statue would swim. It had already come to my attention that any changes to anything—from the brand of coffee served at the local diner to the flowers set in the tubs on the sidewalk—could set off a town-wide panic.

In response to the irritating tinkle, I turned around with the wig still clutched in my hand. Please don't let it be a last-minute customer, I thought. And there stood Kitty. Things were still a little weird following the

Taking Of The Key, but I hoped they'd go back to normal some time soon. Kitty really was a big help, no matter how annoying she could be, and I'd be sad if I lost her.

"Hey, Kitty." Here Kitty, Kitty. Come closer so I can stroke your fur backward.

"Well, hello, Ivy. Closing things up a little late, aren't you?"

Everything she said seemed to come out with a bite, and I was a little tired of it, but I held my tongue. Maybe she was still trying to figure out how to treat the new girl. Besides, the store was mine and nothing would change that, so I could afford to be a little forgiving.

"Just finishing up, Kitty. What brings you here so late? Aren't you going to the Harvest Ball?"

"Of course I'm going to the Ball, silly."

Silly? See what I mean? It came out like "you big freaking idiot."

"So what brings you out to the shop, then?"

"Oh, you know." No, I didn't know and that's why I'd asked. "I was coming to see if I could pick up that adorable bonnet I saw yesterday. I think it'll be a great compliment to my Little House on the Prairie costume."

"Oh, sure. The bonnet is in the back. Let me get it for you." I placed the black wig on the counter next to a royal blue mask and walked into the room directly behind the counter to rummage around in a box of odds and ends.

"So is this the mask you're going to wear, Ivy?"

She'd raised her voice to be heard, so I did the same thing, yelling back, "Yeah, I think it'll look great. How do you like the flapper outfit? Do you think it will bring in more business?"

"Oh, um, of course, dear. You look lovely. I'm surprised you were able to find something so form-fitting in your size."

Thank God I was in the storeroom with my back to her. I really thought I saw red for a minute. How dare she? I turned around to ask her that very question and the look on her face was so innocent, I wondered if I'd misinterpreted what she said. Or was I so bent on showing everyone who was the boss I looked for insults and ways to prove my leadership all the time? Nah. But who cared about why, anyway? I didn't have time to make a comprehensive list of my faults right now. I did take a moment to appreciate the use of "comprehensive." I missed having someone to appreciate big words with me.

Anyway, I still had the Ball to go to and the stolen lingerie thing to figure out. Kitty could say whatever she wanted and however she wanted to say it, because I had better things to do.

I came out, gave her the bonnet, and said a fond farewell instead of kicking her scrawny ass out the door. Score one for Ivy.

I took the wig to its head for a second time and threw the royal blue mask under the counter. I'd do the rest tomorrow, after I woke up from my night of revelry and—dare I hope?—hot monkey love.

The bell tinkled again, and I stifled a sigh. It was probably Kitty again, trying to see when I was really leaving, or throwing another pot shot at me. And I should have been gone already, on my way to a party where I was hoping to cop another feel on Zorro.

But it wasn't Kitty. It was a woman I'd seen a

couple of times around town. I'd heard she was a graphic designer who worked out of her home, and I kept reminding myself I needed to talk to her to get some kind of new advertisement going.

"Janice, right?" I said. Another little piece of business savvy I'd picked up from another trusty book, *Ways to Make A Customer Show Loyalty Like a Faithful Dog*. Remember the customer's name and they'll come back again and again.

"Wow, I'm impressed. Some of my own clients still call me 'girl.' "

We both laughed, and she had one of those light, airy laughs that invited you to join in.

"Yeah, some of the older people here are having a hard time getting past the fact that I'm not over ninety and white-haired, like Gertie. And without the white hair and knee-high stockings, I can't possibly do this shop justice."

"I know exactly what you mean. Us youngsters need to stick together. I haven't had a chance to welcome you to town, Ivy, and I'm really sorry I haven't made the time to come over to introduce myself. I've had this client from out of town—I think he called it Hell." She laughed. "Anyway, he's this big account, so I haven't even seen the light of day in the past two weeks, much less gotten out to say hi to anyone but my dog."

"Don't even worry about it," I said, thinking I might have found myself another friend. But I'd wait to make a final determination. Reference the Jackie Sturder debacle and my lack of good judgment there. Although there was something genuinely nice about Janice that made me feel like we were already friends.

"What can I do for you? Do you need a costume?"

"Yeah. I can't believe I didn't think of it before tonight. But as I said, this guy has been a pain in my ass. Everything I did was right until it came time to send it to the printers, and then he started freaking out on me about tiny color changes and the way certain things were set up. He'd already signed off on everything, but I was trying to keep him happy in case he could send more clients my way. Turns out, all I got for my trouble was a headache." Janice paused and shook her blond head. "Sorry, again. I seem to keep saying that, but this time I feel I'm keeping you, and boring you at the same time."

"Not a problem. You weren't boring me at all. Actually, it's kind of comforting to know I'm not the only one dealing with cranky people." I smiled and knew I was in the process of making another really good friend. I wondered if she ever got together with Bella. We could have some awesome Girls' Nights. "So what's your fancy tonight?"

"I love what you're wearing," she said. "Do you have anything else like it?"

I knew there was a reason why I liked this woman. "Let me see," I said, thinking about the extra flapper costume that hadn't been picked up this afternoon. I doubted the customer who'd ordered it would want it this late into the evening. Besides, I was locking the door right after Janice. Maybe we could go to The Barn together and I wouldn't be left looking like the only wallflower in the place.

"I do have one flapper get-up left. Size twelve, right?"

"You hit it right on the nose," Janice said.

"Just a little leftover skill from my last job." I walked around the counter, picked the costume out of the rack on the left wall, and took Janice back to the dressing rooms. She ducked into the first curtained cubicle, and we talked while she was changing.

Two minutes later, her sweatshirt and old jeans were gone and in their place was a great fringed skirt and a sleeveless top in a cool blue only two shades different from my own. We could have been twins. "You look fantastic." But the hair was all wrong with the colors in the short outfit. I remembered the black wig I'd put away and went to retrieve it.

I helped her tuck all that blond hair up under the wig and grabbed the royal blue mask from under the counter. She put the mask on and looked... "Perfect."

"Thanks so much, Ivy. I really appreciate you helping me out on such short notice." She patted her new 'do and waited while I locked up behind us.

Strolling out onto the main road, the crisp autumn air swirled the fallen leaves from the flower tubs and gutters, cleaning the street and making me long for a steaming cup of apple cider. This is what fall was supposed to be like, not the all-the-time sunshine of southern California. I loved this town and wanted to stay for as long as they'd have me.

Now I had to get through my first small-town shindig and continue to make a good impression. No embarrassing moments of drunken stumbling, no dancing on tables (as if I'd ever done that), and no hot and heavy action with Ben, at least not on the dance floor. But no one said I couldn't take him home.

Nothing would go wrong tonight, not with Bella already there and Janice as my new ally.

Life was good. I had a great new career, a possible lover, and two great new friends. Everything was going much better than I'd expected on the day I opened that letter and read the words "your inheritance."

My only problem was I kept on waiting for the proverbial other shoe to drop. Nothing had ever been this easy for me. Why did I think everything would fall into place this time? I didn't know, and I was soon to find out that the other shoe was not merely a shoe, but a woman's size eleven with a stiletto heel.

Chapter Seven

Luminaries made from sand-filled paper bags lined the circular gravel drive in front of the barn. I'd followed Janice's little green Miata to the Ball because I wanted to be able to leave on my own (or with Ben in tow) at the end of the evening. Tomorrow was going to be a busy one for me—all those costume returns. Yikes!

But I banished the thought to the back of my mind as I parked my Hyundai and waited for Janice to finish her makeup in the Miata's rearview mirror. I checked my little black handbag to make sure I had all the essentials for the evening: wallet, license, new cell phone Bella had programmed, against my repeated protests, to play an annoying rendition of James Brown when it rang.

I took the phone out of my bulging purse and attached it to my waist to eke out a little more room for the blood-red lipstick and the perfume I'd chosen for tonight. Might need to touch up, if my plans for kissing Ben came to fruition. (*Another good word. Must remember to throw it at Daisy, Maggie, Rose, and Dad during one of our weekly calls.*)

When Janice finally emerged from her car, I was anxious to get into the Barn and see if my visions of Zorro matched the way Ben filled out the costume in real life. Would I do a graceful swan dive to the floor upon seeing him? At least that would get my fear of embarrassing myself out of the way quick.

After putting on our masks, Janice and I walked up to the big double doors and the funny thing was that, for the first time in a long time, I found someone who could match my stride. My legs weren't really long, but I tended to be a fast walker and had found myself ten feet ahead of Bella the couple of times we'd walked around town. It was refreshing to have someone who could keep up.

"So what kind of dancing do you have at these things?" I asked her as we walked through the enormous doors and gave our coats to a skinny girl in a witch's hat and cape from my shop. *Thank you, skinny girl.* "Am I going to be looked down on because I don't know how to do-si-do?"

Janice laughed and lightly swatted me on the arm. "For God's sake," she said, "we're not hicks."

We'd agreed not to use our names yet because we wanted to stay anonymous for a little while before we had to do the whole mingling thing. Janice had told me this was one of the best places to drum up business for the remainder of the year. Most people needed annual reports and Christmas cards done and were still looking for someone to help them. So Janice helped by passing out her business card and reminding them she was local and available.

"I wasn't thinking hick." Had I already offended my potential new friend? It would be just like me. Open mouth insert high heel. "I thought square dancing was popular here and didn't want to be caught unaware."

"Yeah, right. You are so full of crap. But I dare you to request 'The Virginia Reel' before the night's over." A smile and a wink told me I had not in fact shoved my foot in my mouth. Good.

We made our way into the main room, and my eyes took a minute to adjust to the lack of fluorescent light. Even though I was being hustled along the length of the cement floor of the hall, I took the time to study my surroundings and get a feel for the place. Large, old-fashioned chandeliers filled with pillar candles hung from exposed beams, orange and black tealight candles floated in mini cauldrons filled with green-tinted water, and candelabras draped with spider webs had been placed on each round table circling the scarred wood dance floor.

We arrived at the food tables and accepted smoking punch in pumpkin mugs from a ghoul. I was a little afraid to go see what they had for food. The town obviously took this Halloween business seriously. I hoped I wouldn't be forced to make my excuses over bat soup or eye of newt on toast points—caviar was bad enough. Ew! Then again, this was technically the country, so I assumed I should worry more about something that involved cow tongue or chicken livers.

"So how long do these things usually last?" I asked Janice as we stood at the base of the darkened stage situated in the far corner of the cavernous barn.

"Until about eleven. Why? Hot date?"

"I seriously hope so, if my fantasy comes true with Zorro."

"Zorro?" she said, but then I didn't have a chance to elaborate, because a man dressed as Robin Hood came up and grabbed Janice's hand to slobber all over it. Janice tugged it out of his grasp and giggled after Sir Robin of the funky hood, which could not have come from my shop because it was too tacky, finally kissed every finger on her hand.

The no-names thing made introductions awkward, but we made do with, "Hi, friend of Janice," and a return, "Nice to meet you, friend of Janice also." I knew Janice didn't mean to not include me in their conversation, but somehow they started talking about something called Bluelines, and I started looking around for someone else so I could make their acquaintance. Plus, I was still keeping an eye out for the elusive Zorro.

I spotted Bella in her trampy princess costume and tapped Janice on the shoulder. "I'm going to go talk to that princess," I mouthed.

"Okay," she mouthed back and squeezed my hand. "I'll see you later."

I took off in the direction where I'd last seen Princess Trasherella and found her near a huge barrel smelling of apples and cinnamon. We hugged and she whispered, "You look fabulous. Not a spot of brown in sight. I'm so proud of you. Tell me your underwear is some exotic color."

"Isn't that supposed to be some lucky stud's line?" I asked.

"Har-har. Now answer the question."

"They're brown," I said with a straight face. The look she gave me in return was simply priceless.

"No way. You have to be joking." She stared into my eyes like she was willing me to come up with a different answer. "Tell me you are joking."

"You sure are pretty demanding with your 'tell me's.' "

"Don't toy with me, Ivy Morris. Are you or are you not wearing something other than brown underneath that fabulous costume?" Her voice became louder with every word.

"Yes, Ivy." My skin prickled with goose bumps as someone whispered in my ear. "Tell us what you have under that fabulous costume."

Holy crap! I whirled to find Ben stood directly behind me in all his dark, mysterious hero glory. The black hat sat at a rakish angle over brown hair just visible under the brim. A black silk shirt hung open to the middle of a magnificent chest touched with enough hair to play with post-coitally. Black shiny pants hugged muscles and flesh like a second skin. A black satin cape swirled to the backs of his knees, where it met the top of his polished boots. The mask added to the overall yummy factor, and my mouth started to water. Seriously, it was a true test of my mettle as a woman to not start panting like a bitch in heat.

I did not want to go back to wishing the floor would open up and swallow me whole, so I tried something new. Brash and brazen—the hussy flapper. "Actually, you'll be pleased to know that this night's underwear choice is purple velvet."

Bella smiled, and I was pretty sure I'd managed to shut Ben up for the first time in his life. No sexy comments, no snappy comeback—just his mouth hanging open wide enough to catch flies.

I took it a step further, raised my upturned hand to gently rest it beneath his chin, and closed his mouth with a snap. He jerked out of his stupefaction (*Oh, good word, Ivy*) and I saw him try to work up a suitable response. I headed him off at the pass. "Later, Boy Wonder, I might let you find out how incredibly soft velvet can be." Then I walked away, pulling a laughing

Bella behind me.

"You are so bad." Bella snickered for about the fifth time as we made our way slowly through the buffet-style food line. Cream puffs and little quiches sat next to something called succotash and a big crockpot of baked beans. Not exactly what I had imagined for a Harvest Ball, but I was willing to embrace different.

We found a place to sit after our plates were full. Our candelabra's candles stood tall and straight, barely used in all their orange glory. Fortunately, they didn't have a pumpkin scent or some other essence associated with Halloween. I did not want to try to eat my fragrant French dip while inhaling a burning leaves smell, thank you very much.

"That was pretty steamy with Ben," Bella said, spooning up some potato salad. "Are you really thinking about taking him to bed already?"

"Yes and no." I sighed because theory was always so much better than reality. In theory, I could take Ben to bed and not need some kind of commitment from him. In theory, I could have my way with him, leave in the middle of the night, and take him or leave him the next day. In theory, I wasn't terrified I'd be the one left the next day without a phone call, dreaming of our wedding and tearing through one of those baby books looking for names for our three children.

In reality, I knew I'd never sleep with him until we'd been on at least three dates. It was a personal rule for a reason, but that didn't mean I couldn't tease him in the process.

"Yes, I'd love to be able to take him home and have my way with him. But no, I've never done that and I can't see myself starting now."

"Come on, Ivy. You could do it. Lure him back to your love nest and let nature take its course." She speared a carrot and popped it into her red-slicked mouth.

"You have got to be kidding me." I watched in amazement. Her lipstick didn't fade one bit with each new piece of food she put in her mouth. How did she do that? "How do you do that?" I shook my head. "Never mind. I liked Ben when I met him. He's fun, and sexy as hell, but I need more than that. I, uh, can't get into the, uh, mood if I don't have pretty strong feelings for someone." And why was I talking about my sex life in the middle of the second biggest party of the year? (Christmas being number one.) I was talking about my sex life in the middle of the second biggest party of the year because this was Bella, and ever since we'd both choked on the coloring fumes coming from my hair in her salon, I've felt I could tell her anything.

But with Zorro lingering in the area, I had to be very careful with what I said. He seemed to be right next to my ear every time I said anything the least bit risqué. I quickly looked around the huge room and my eyes landed on the broadest shoulders I'd ever had the pleasure of touching. The cape still draped over the shoulders, but my mind kept conjuring up this awesome image of all that yummy flesh uncovered before my very eyes. At least I was sitting down, so no one had to witness my knees turning to Jell-O when he turned around and his eyes locked on mine, the wicked smile washing across his chiseled face again.

Totally swoon worthy. And speaking of worthy, did I really think this guy seriously wanted me for more than a roll in the proverbial hay, when he was as god-like as Adonis? I mean, little kids didn't run away from me screaming, but surely he could find someone else more his physical equal, even in a town this small. The point became moot when Bella dug her nails into my arm and said, "Here comes Kitty."

I'd told Bella about the weird feeling I got when Kitty talked to me. I'd kept the lingerie theft to myself, however, because it was going to be my first foray into the land of backbone. Could I figure out who the thief was, and would I stand up to him or her when I had their name? There were no guarantees I'd have the brass balls to do it, but I was certainly going to attempt to channel my inner Bella and try.

Kitty glided right past us, and I was a little baffled. Had I been snubbed, or did she really not recognize me?

"Can you believe that?" Bella asked. "You should march right up to her and tell her to never ignore you like that again."

I thought about it for maybe a second and then came to a decision. "You know, I'm going to pass on that. If she doesn't want to talk to me, it's no skin off my nose. Actually, it'll be nice to not listen to her make her thinly veiled, snide comments for one evening. Besides, she looks kind of distracted, doesn't she? Like she has something on her mind?"

"What, other than her perfectly done steel hair and her precious son, could possibly fit in her little head?"

"That's not very nice, Bella."

She took a sip of her punch and eyed me over the rim. "Why do you care? She's so fake and mean. Did I ever tell you about the time she went ballistic in the salon because I gave her tea with sugar instead of

Sweet-N-Low? Turns out she says her body can't tolerate sugar. I got a huge nasty lecture from her. Witch. I don't know how Jackie puts up with her as a potential mother-in-law. Charlie must be a freaking wonder in bed."

I didn't have an answer for her, so I went back to ogling the object of my near-affection, wondering if he was worthy of a witchy mother-in-law because of his prowess in bed. I bet he was.

That object breathed into my ear a split-second after I smelled his dark cologne. What was it about my ears? He always breathed or whispered into them. I would have asked, but I didn't want him to think I was uncomfortable and decide to stop. I loved the delicious shiver that ran through my body whenever he did the ear-whispering thing. Plus, was there a tactful way to say, "You can't talk in my ear but I wouldn't object to a little nibbling"? There was the Hussy Flapper again, raring to come back out and play. I'd have to remember to spritz my eau-de-toilet behind my earlobes from now on.

"Hey, Velvet. Care to dance?"

Okay, a serious tremor streaked down my back, darting to my stomach and lower. Now, I could do one of two things at this point. I could a) turn my head slightly and brush my lips against his as I said a sultry "yes," or b) worry about my breath since I took that bite of spicy potato salad with the onion in it.

Yeah, I chose "b." I'm not dumb.

In answer to Zorro's question and avoidance of the potential bad-breath issue, I pushed my chair back and stood up. A discreet hand over my mouth and one quick exhale informed me the breath wasn't as bad as I thought. I immediately felt better about the prospect of snuggling up to my favorite folklore hero and sexy food critic.

After leading me out to the scarred wooden dance floor, his big hands circled around my waist and rested on the curves of my hips. He slowly drew me closer to his chest, and I was gratified to find myself nestled under his chin, even with the added height of my spike heels. Very nice.

Eric Clapton crooned "You Look Wonderful Tonight" and Zorro sang it in my ear in a horrible Spanish accent. It could have been a really romantic moment, but it struck me as incredibly funny, which got me even hotter than just sexy. There's something about a guy who doesn't take himself too seriously and doesn't expect you to take him seriously all the time, either.

We moved around the polished floor in a tight circle. Avoiding the other couples on the floor wasn't difficult, given the fact Ben pretty much shuffled his feet back and forth and held me close. Although that wasn't a very good description of Ben's dancing abilities, because he also had this whole pelvic motion thing that was both distracting and ecstasy-producing at the same time. I felt hypnotized when I moved my head from his chest and looked up into his clear green eyes. A spell was coming over me, and it was exciting. My only problem was that I couldn't figure out if I wanted to be powerless against it or stick to my own rules and ruin what I was sure would be a great time for myself. The decision was torn right out of my hands as a scream ripped through the barn.

Chapter Eight

I jerked away from Ben, startled at the scream. Then I felt the vibrating at my waist and remembered my damn cell phone. The one with the new ring tone Bella had so thoughtfully put on it. Nothing like the scream of James Brown during "I Feel Good" to stop you from potentially getting as close to a wonderful set of lips as possible.

"Dammit," I said, fumbling for the infernal phone so I could at least turn off the loop of the song. I teetered on my extremely high heels (that made my legs look extra sexy but did nothing for my poor sore feet) until Ben grabbed my elbow and steered me to the edge of the dance floor.

Flipping open the phone, I looked at the digital readout and groaned when I saw it was Bella. "Yes, Bella? Why are you calling me when we're in the same room?"

She snorted. "As if you didn't know. I'm saving you from yourself. Things were looking a little steamy with you and Ben, and I wanted to stop you from making a mistake."

"You have got to be kidding me."

"I absolutely am not kidding you. I saw that wily hand of his creeping down to your ass and your fingers playing with the neckline of his fabulous hair, and decided to jump in, but not in an intrusive way."

"You don't find this intrusive?"

"Not compared to physically insinuating myself between the two of you. I guess I could have come over and moved his hand back up to the middle of your back where it should have stayed in the first place. Or maybe I could have smacked your hand while it played with the hair on his neck. Either way, I thought this was the better option."

Damn cell phones and their innate ability to make you available to any loon who has your number and wants to get in touch with you. A perfectly good moment had been ruined, all because I'd been waiting for a call from my father and so had brought the phone with me in the first place. Although, on the other hand, I much preferred being interrupted by Bella than my dad, who had always been able to tell when I was doing something he wouldn't approve of. On the third hand, I was twenty-four and wandering hands were part and parcel of being a sexually active adult, which was what I eventually wanted to be with Ben.

"I don't really need a keeper, Bella. I'm capable of handling myself." I whispered the last part because Ben was taking an inordinate amount of interest in my conversation.

"Of course you need a keeper. Even from all the way across the room, I could see your eyes getting all dewy and droopy with that latent lust thing. I bet you would have been naked by now if you two had been in a room without all these people around."

"That is so not true," I said, a little louder than I meant to and had several heads turn my way. I lowered the volume of my voice. "Look, I know what I'm doing, and it's not nearly getting naked."

"Are you sure?" The words were whispered in my other ear. Ben, entering my conversation when he was least wanted, as always.

"Hey, what are you doing?" I backed away from Ben and his eternal, goose-bump-raising whispers.

"What do you mean, what am I doing? I told you, trying to save you from yourself. And why is Ben in your ear again? Did you put some kind of special perfume back there that he's drawn to?"

I was not going to tell her that was precisely what I had done on one of my trips to the ladies' room. I was not that stupid.

The distance separating Ben from me diminished when he grabbed my free hand and started kissing my knuckles. "I'm going now, Bella. Thanks for the Mom moment." I hung up and endured Ben's laughter while I tried to get the cell phone hooked back into its holder at my waist.

"Ha, ha, Ben. Shut up." I yanked my hand out of his grasp and gave him my best "you're a shit" look.

Once he composed himself and stopped acting like a snorting high school freshman, he apologized, but the mood was ruined. Bella had served her purpose. Dammit again. I guess I wasn't doing so hot on the whole not-swearing thing.

I stalked off to the punch table and grabbed up a mini cauldron of steaming apple cider. Stupid men and their stupid laughing, I thought. Ben could take his sense of humor and...and... Well, I didn't know, but when I came up with something suitably, appropriately horrible, I would let him know.

I started looking around for someone to talk to, since I was no longer talking to Ben and maybe not even Bella. I didn't need a keeper and I didn't need an idiot who thought he could take up where he left off after he embarrassed me. So I looked for Janice. She would be nice and not laugh at my expense. She wouldn't check up on me like I was a child. And, hopefully, she would tolerate my out-of-whack foul mood until I settled down.

Asking other partygoers if they'd seen Janice was easier when people didn't know who I was. The mask covered half my face, so I didn't get the attitude I'd previously experienced in town. The last person I asked told me she'd seen Janice go behind the thick red velvet curtain obscuring the stage.

I pushed the curtain aside and slipped behind it. Immediately, I was hit by the musty smell of cardboard and dust. There was very little light back here, but I did see a faint glow coming from a corridor behind another curtain, this one black. Although it could have been orange, for all I knew, it was that dark back here.

The clack of my heels rang extremely loudly on the hard wooden stage. I didn't realize how loudly until the noise stopped and I was left listening only to my own breathing. This was getting a little weird. The farther I moved into the stage area, the more muffled outside sound became.

I wove my way around big scene boards filled with trees and rolling hills, past boxes overflowing with props, and around a huge potted plant. One of the silky leaves brushed against my bare arm and it took me a moment to control my pounding heart. "Just a tree, just a tree," I whispered to myself, since there didn't seem to be any other living thing back here.

For some reason I started hearing the theme from

Psycho ringing in my ears. On the surface there was nothing to be scared of back here, but something was making my skin crawl. A nebulous something. I laughed at the tension I felt and congratulated myself on another good word. Unfortunately, that wasn't working either. Something was wrong. I could feel it down to the toes of my reinforced pantyhose.

More silence greeted me when I finally came to the door with the only light under it. I listened, my ear against the wood for a moment. I did not want to interrupt some assignation Janice had set up for herself, or barge into a meeting. Though why someone would set up a meeting back here in the dark was beyond me.

My cursory nod to appropriate behavior over, I knocked. No noise came from behind the closed door, so I tried again. "Hello?" I said. "Anybody in there?"

Again no answer came, so I thought about turning around and looking for Janice elsewhere. But a niggling little voice in my head kept telling me something was on the other side of that door. Combined with the lack of a response from said side of the door, my natural curiosity was aroused, and I tried again, this time jiggling the handle to the door.

"Hello? Anyone?" Should I break down the door? But that sounded ridiculous. I mean, anything could be going on inside the room. Who said there weren't people in there who were ignoring me because they had no clothes on and were going at it like wild animals? Although wild animals usually made some kind of noise and I was still hearing nothing. I jiggled the doorknob again, and this time the door popped open.

Once my eyes adjusted to the light, after its absence in the backstage area, I barely held back a scream to rival that of Mr. James Brown. There on the floor, in a very unnatural position, was the one person I'd been looking for. The one I thought would tolerate me in my bad mood. The friend I had hoped to make and keep and add to my very small collection in a town that was not turning out to be the friendliest place for out-of-towners. And maybe not for towners, either, since Janice, in all her flapper glory, lay at the foot of a grape-colored sofa with blood crusted on the front of her sequined top.

Chapter Nine

It was like a slow-motion moment in a weird dream. My hand moved in minute increments to touch the skin at Janice's throat. I'd watched enough television to know you checked for a pulse before you started screaming the house down.

Thoughts pinged through my head: maybe the blood was fake, maybe my fingers would register a thump, thump, thump that would tell me Janice had fainted or was taking a nap. Unlikely, as there was no thump, thump, thump under my fingertips, the rational part of my brain told me, but I couldn't wrap my head around the fact that Janice was really, really dead.

Dead. "Aaaaaahhhhhhh!"

Once my initial scream worked its way from the bottom of my uncomfortable shoes, through my chest, and out of my mouth, I started hyperventilating. The breath whooshed in and out of my lungs in great, gulping gasps. I stumbled away from Janice's inert body, shaking and shivering, as I tried to back through the solid wall behind me. Since that was physically impossible, I folded my arms over my chest and felt my stomach roll dangerously.

What if the killer was somewhere in the area? I hadn't even thought of that initially, and here I was standing alone in the backstage area of a barn I'd never been to before, in a town that hadn't been very friendly to me, three thousand miles away from my friends and family.

My ears didn't pick up any ringing footsteps in the hallway in front of the room, so I whipped out my cell phone and dialed the last number who called me.

"Bella," I said as soon as the ringing stopped. I didn't even give her a chance to say hello. "I need your help."

"Sorry," she said, snide and pouty, "I'm not in the mood to give you another Mom moment. You'll have to survive on your own." And she hung up.

Holy shit. I so did not have the time for a pouty party. I speed-dialed this time and waited through seven rings before she answered again.

"What?" she said, her tone flat.

"Look, I don't have time for this, Bella. I'm backstage and we have a serious problem. I think Janice is dead, and nobody can hear me screaming back here. Can you please, please, find the police chief or whoever and send them behind the curtain before I pass out or become the next victim."

Bella gasped and then hung up on me again, but I hoped this time she took me seriously and was looking for the local fuzz. I really kicked up the hopeful wishing a notch when I heard footsteps pounding on the floor outside. Please, God, let that be the police and not the killer come back to kill another someone. Come back to kill me.

The footsteps sounded like a herd of shoppers at a Robinson's May One-Day Sale. I stepped back from the door a split second before it was thrown open and a tall man charged in, dressed as a medieval knight.

He was not alone, which I knew from the stampede

noises, but I was surprised at how many people filled the narrow doorway. Like some kind of human tidal wave, they streamed in behind the knight, and the small room felt overly crowded as people pushed and shoved their way forward to see the body. The whispering started immediately.

"Who is that?"

"What happened?"

"Is she dead?"

Until the knight stalked up to the body and cleared a wide circle merely by clearing his throat. Everyone else got the message. I guess the throat clearing was some kind of signal I, as a new resident, did not pick up on.

"Move it, move it," he barked as he came closer and I still hadn't moved. I found myself getting roughly pushed out of the way.

"Excuse me," Sir Pushy said, sarcasm edging his voice. Clearly I was not moving fast enough or far enough. But really, where could I go with all these people in the room?

"Sorry." I tried to stay pleasant even though I still shivered from being in the room so close to a dead Janice. Whoever this guy was, I was sure I didn't want to piss him off.

"Ma'am, you'll need to move over with the others."

Ma'am? I wasn't old enough to be a ma'am. But I tried to move anyway. The medieval knight exuded a kind of don't-mess-with-me authority.

"All right, you people need to get the hell out of this room." This man would never need a bullhorn. "But don't leave the building until you've spoken to one of my officers."

And everybody did just that, except one woman who had pushed to the front, as others were retreating, and promptly fainted at the feet of a pirate complete with a parrot on his shoulder. He'd picked that outfit from my costume shop, very classy get-up. Although why I was thinking of the costume shop at a time like this was beyond me.

****

I sat down hard on a chair festooned with fall-colored leaves and stared at the burnt-orange tablecloth. The raised swirling patterns on the cloth caught and held my attention as Bella sank into a chair to my left while Ben leaned on the edge of the table. He was probably looking sexy in his nonchalant way, but I couldn't even process the scene I'd staggered away from ten minutes ago, much less appreciate Ben's appeal.

My new friend was dead. The wonderful woman, the one I'd sold a flapper costume to and laughed over difficult clients with, was gone.

After Sir Pushy—who I found out was our police chief—had leaned down to check for a pulse and came up shaking his head, he'd ordered everyone back into the main hall and away from the backstage area. My last sight of Janice was right before a forest green blanket settled over her sequined sleeveless top and black wig. I couldn't keep the image from flashing across my brain. Every time I closed my eyes, it was like a projector stuck on three seconds of film. Blanket whooshes open and drifts through the air, settling on Janice. And then it started all over again.

Someone was kind enough to hand me a glass of

punch, and I cupped it, without drinking, as I worked my way through the scene a fifth time. I couldn't believe vital, energetic, happy Janice was gone. About that time, I started to cry.

Gone.

Gone forever while I'd been thinking about taking a bite out of Ben and he'd been sliding his hands down my back on his way to my behind. What a horrible, horrible thing. I couldn't get my mind around it. God, I couldn't believe this was happening.

Bella grabbed my hand and sobbed, "What is the world coming to when Janice is dead? And dressed like some kind of showgirl, too?"

I snapped out of my stupor. "She was *not* a showgirl. She was a flapper, like me." Young like me, too. I thought it, but didn't say it out loud.

The police chief and two officers came around and interviewed everyone. After the questioning, people started trickling out through the massive double doors, headed home. Without a doubt, the grapevine was about to be set on fire.

Ben was nice enough to follow me the two miles home. Only briefly did I think about inviting him in to give release to the tumultuous feelings clamoring inside me after seeing death close up. But even my freshly shaved legs—and the feeling they were going to waste—couldn't make me want to seriously contemplate being with anyone, much less intimately, right now. I wanted to put on sweatpants and a sweatshirt, get a hot cup of tea, find my cozy bed. And some time to grieve, even though I'd only known Janice for a matter of hours.

Of course, Ben insisted on coming in to check the

house before he would let me lock him out. So I put on a kettle of water while Ben stalked his way through the kitchen. I waited for the water to boil as he checked out the rest of the house.

"All clear," he said in a pretty good imitation of someone who actually knew what they were doing. Then again, I'd forgotten about the PI license he had via the Internet. Maybe they showed you, with a virtual walk-through, how to accomplish making sure a home was safe. I was getting punchy if I was back to picking on the PI license. To overcome the guilt of my petty thought, I put a lot of warmth into my tired voice when I said, "Thanks, Ben, for looking through the house for me. I feel better now."

"Not a problem. This wasn't exactly the ending I'd envisioned for this evening," he said.

"Yeah, me neither."

He traced a circular pattern on the back of my hand. The teakettle whistled and I jumped about a foot in the air. "Crap!" I yelled, my hand going to my racing heart. I apologized for the outburst in a more normal tone.

"No, it's okay. I think we're both a little jumpy right now. Will you be able to sleep tonight?"

Yes. No. Yes. No. I came out with, "Yea-no."

He laughed a little. "Is that a maybe?"

I gave a little laugh of my own. "It's a yeah. I'll be fine, thanks for asking. I really appreciate you going out of your way to see me home."

"Believe me, it wasn't a hardship."

"Well, thanks all the same."

"So does my knight-in-shining-armor routine get me dinner with you?"

"How can you be a knight in shining armor when you're dressed as Zorro?" I asked. All right, I was trying for coy and not doing a very good job, but I did get another chuckle out of him.

"Would you agree to savior in black shiny pants? How about protector in long flapping cape? Guardian in a great hat?"

"How about you stop before I kick you out for stupid jokes?"

He gave me a lopsided grin that reminded me of the puppy, Jackson, I'd had when I was about ten. He'd eat my best pair of shoes and then turn on the charm. It always worked because I was a sucker for bad boys in trouble. And this smile was seriously lethal, but I'd girded myself against lethal early this evening. Yes, Ben was sexy, and funny, and sexy, and charming. And don't forget sexy. But was he really for me? Did I want to throw myself at the first eligible guy who crossed my path? Didn't I have more self-worth than that? Didn't I have scruples? What did I really know about Ben, other than surface information? Virtually nothing. And I was a little uncomfortable with the answer of virtually nothing.

But dinner? I could definitely go for dinner. I mean, what the heck? "I suppose I could pencil you into my busy schedule for a dinner sometime next week. What night?" Was that me who'd just been pro-active *and* forward? Woohoo! Go, me! I was proud of myself, until I realized Ben was still standing in front of me. Staring. "What?" I said. "Do I have something in my teeth? On my face?"

"No. I'm admiring the view."

"Puh-lease."

"Seriously. You look stunning."

"Oh, ah, I, um." I still wore the whole flapper costume but had removed the black satin and sequin mask.

"Ivy Morris, speechless? Impossible. I'm shocked." With a smug smile growing on his face, he leaned against the corner of the square oak table and crossed his muscular arms over an impressive chest.

My mouth went dry, and it felt like my tongue swelled to outrageous proportions. The one good thing here was I couldn't open my mouth to make some stupid remark that would only make me look bad. I spent a few seconds doing a poor imitation of a guppy without the water. And then, when I got the power of speech back, I came out with the most inane thing I'd probably ever uttered.

"Knock it off," I said, cringing inside, because really, who did I think I was? I'd never been a straight-shooting, smart-talking chick. My personality leaned more toward mousy, quiet, introverted. Did I seriously think my whole personality would change because I was on the other side of the country?

A small part of my mind yelled at me for my ridiculous crap. I could be whoever I wanted to be. Regardless of the past, I was making my own future. No one had to know who I used to be, only who I wanted to be.

"Knock it off? Is that the best you can do? I expected better from you." The full-fledged smile came out, but with a little more devilry in it. It made a previously unnoticed (and I thought I had catalogued his whole body) dimple pop out on his left cheek.

He was too yummy for words, and my inner chick

was crying to be let out. So I did the one thing I knew would shut him and his mocking up. I stepped forward in my brightly lit kitchen, with its gingham drapes and ancient appliances, and kissed him.

Chapter Ten

And what a kiss it was. Now, just because I hadn't been on a date in a while didn't mean I'd forgotten what it was like to be kissed. But I had never, in all my life, been kissed so thoroughly that the roots of my hair tingled.

Ben's lips played over mine a brief second after I initiated the kiss. His firm mouth pressed down on mine, taking me a level deeper than I was prepared for when I started the whole thing. My lips parted and his tongue took the opportunity to explore.

I lost my breath and couldn't have cared less, but my lungs had other ideas. I broke the kiss with a gasp and stumbled back. My expression must have had a tinge of panic to it, because Ben rubbed a long, broad hand up and down my arm in a soothing motion, like I was about to bolt at any second. He wasn't far from the truth.

"That was, um...nice," I said.

The beast had the gall to laugh. "Nice? I was going to say outstanding, but I suppose nice is better than awful."

I knew I was blushing, and that didn't help my discomfort. I'd been kissed like never before and I came out with "nice." No wonder I hadn't had a relationship in a few years. I was a certifiable idiot. I barely managed to stop myself from slapping my head.

"It was better than nice, okay? Surely you know you're a great kisser. You don't need me to stroke your ego."

"Well, maybe not my ego..."

What, were we in high school? "What, are we in high school?" I said my thought out loud before I'd taken the time to process it. Must remember to work on that damn mouth filter.

He didn't even have the grace to look sheepish. "No, we aren't. But we can pretend, if it'll make it better for you." He paused, working his left eyebrow up and down. Very sexy when I was trying to be very cool. "Hey, Ivy, want to go for a ride in my car to Lover's Lane where we can neck?"

"Ha, ha. Get out of my house, you idiot."

"That's no way to talk to the man of your wet dreams, is it?"

"You sure are full of yourself," I said.

"Well, when you're the best, you don't have to hide your light under a bushel."

That sounded eerily close to what I was thinking the first night I'd met him, which was all of forty-eight hours ago. I was so not having sex with this man until I figured out who he was and why he was interested in me.

"Good night, Ben," I said as I pushed him through the house and opened the front door. Brisk air blew in through the opening, bringing with it the smell and feel of autumn: burning leaves and chilly nights.

He took his coat from the stand in the hall and walked backward out the door. His smile was a mile wide and had a smug lift at the corner. I was torn between never letting him near me again, because of the smugness, and running after him to drag him back so I could have my way with him, because of the incredible power of that same smile.

Stand firm, Ivy, I told myself, staying in the doorway as he gracefully descended the one step to the front walkway. I had kind of entertained a quick vision of him tripping and ruining his smooth exit, but he made it down the walk, onto the curb, and to his Explorer without incident. Rounding the hood of the black vehicle, he got in. Once he'd cranked the ignition, he put down the window and leaned over the passenger seat. I was still standing in the cold air without a jacket, not wanting to watch him go but unable to take the leap and ask him to stay the night.

"Sleep tight," Ben said through the lowered window of the idling car.

"Yeah, thanks for following me home."

"It was all my pleasure. And I hope yours, too." Okay, that was kind of smarmy. Things like that came out of his mouth and immediately made me wonder why I was even interested in him.

"Here's an idea. Think about where you want to go to dinner and let me know," he said, either oblivious to, or ignoring, the wrinkling of my nose. "I'll take care of everything else. Then you be ready on your doorstep at seven sharp on Thursday and open to the possibilities of us having a great time together."

"I'll let you know," I said, as he started putting the window back up.

"Hey," I yelled, and a cloud of white drifted out of my mouth as my words hit the cold air. He made a great big production of leaning across the console and lowering the passenger side window again. "I don't know any restaurants. And with all your experience as a food critic, shouldn't you pick where we're going?" I hated the pressure of picking the right restaurant. What if I chose one that sucked, or worse, one that was too expensive for him? I mean, the guy had an Explorer, but it looked like it had more than a few miles on it. And what about fancy or not fancy? God, so many choices, and I really did not want the responsibility. I might have been growing out of my introverted lifestyle and making progress with my fear of confrontation, but I thought choosing a restaurant was still way down on the syllabus of things I needed to learn for the new and improved Ivy. I knew it was a silly fear. I could choose and that would be the end of it, not care what kind of impression I'd made with my choice. But it seemed a little beyond me right now.

"You're taking the fun out of this," he said, and I stiffened until he continued. "I wanted to make you squirm about the kind of restaurant you chose. I pictured you going through all my past articles and finding out which ones I reviewed favorably and spending a lot of time thinking about me when you did your research."

Well, shit, I guess I could have done that and avoided all the angst of choices. And it would have been a great way to let him know I liked him enough to spend time looking up his articles.

Then again, on the other hand, I probably would have spent all weekend hunting down his articles, nervous he would see me as some kind of stalker for going to the library and looking him up. *Why, oh, why, do I have to be so damn wishy-washy?*

Anyway, he was still sitting in his car with the

window down, and I was still outside without a coat, so I said, "I'll think of you this week, but you pick out the restaurant. And I want to be impressed, so make it good."

"You got it, Ivy. Nothing but the best for my glossy, thriving, trailing plant." He rolled up the window quicker than I'd ever seen anyone use a crank turn, his laughter fading as the glass rolled closed. He waved, and with a roaring of the powerful engine, he was gone.

I bumped into the coat rack as I tried to keep his taillights in sight and close the door at the same time. He wanted me to think of him. He wanted me to be impressed. He was driving me insane, and after only two days.

His trailing plant. Was that a compliment or a comment on where he thought I belonged, behind him? Then again, he did say glossy and thriving. Was thriving a play on my uh...voluptuousness?

Was I reading him wrong? So many questions and so few answers. I felt like I was on a quiz show with a host who had dyslexia. Heaven help me, I'd have to be very careful or I could be in for some serious trouble of the male kind.

I decided to be flattered by the trailing, thriving, glossy reference. The floaty feeling that nothing could bring me down from the high of Ben's kiss stayed with me while I locked up the house and went into my bedroom to get ready for bed. It was one of those exciting feelings that made you do things you didn't exactly want your friends or your potential lover to see you doing. Like waltzing around the house à la Cinderella pre-ball dancing lessons.

But I was alone, so I pseudo-waltzed my heart out. One-two-three, flip the light switch. One-two-three, down the short hall to the bedroom. One-two-three, trip over the shoes I'd left in the middle of the floor earlier today. But I recovered quickly and saved myself from an intimate meeting with the floor.

I'd heard a new dance studio was opening in town two weeks from now; maybe I'd give some serious consideration to lessons. After all, how hard could it be? And I couldn't have Ben be the only one in this (dare I say) relationship who had any sense of balance.

Tugging a pair of sweatpants and a faded, holey sweatshirt (another thing you do not want your friends or potential lover to see you in) over my body, I brushed out my hair and did the whole removing-copious-amounts-of-makeup thing. I wore some blush and eyeliner on most days, but tonight I'd gone all out with concealer and face powder, deep red lipstick, and glitter eye shadow. No way was I going to bed without removing all that pore-clogging junk. I had enough trouble without waking up to a pimple the size of a pea on my oversensitive forehead.

The phone rang as I was brushing my teeth. Mouth full of minty-fresh toothpaste, I scrambled for the receiver, but the ringing stopped before I could click the On button. Which meant I might have sent Ben to voicemail hell after the best kiss of my life. I took a few seconds and rinsed my mouth of said minty freshness and then called the number to check my new messages.

I was all prepared for Ben's sexy voice to tell me what a wonderful night he'd had or that he wanted to move the date up to Tuesday because he couldn't wait to see me alone. Even "Let's have brunch tomorrow" would have made me happy. Which of course went against everything I'd told myself up to this point, i.e., go slow, get to know him, find out the important stuff before I jump into a serious relationship. What I got was a far cry from any of my dream messages. In fact, it was a severely harsh thump back to reality and the parts of the night my mind had shut away when Ben's lips had locked with mine.

"Ivy Morris," a scary and deep voice said over the line. "Hell hath no fury like a woman scorned. Get out and get away before the fury comes down on you. Do you want to end up like your friend?" There was a click like a shutter on an old camera and then the nice, familiar, female voice informed me I could choose to delete this message by pressing the number seven or save it by pressing the number two.

I spent a second with my finger hovering over the seven because the voice scared me. But I collected myself and pressed two to save it, thinking it was cryptic but it could mean something. And I didn't want to throw away a piece of evidence. Evidence against what, I wasn't sure. Janice's death? A message to someone else after my own death? Is that what the caller had meant?

I felt a chill pass over my flesh as my voicemail played the first saved message and the scary voice repeated its spooky words. Slamming down the receiver, I cut the message off but could not silence the voice reverberating in my head.

A friend had died tonight. Janice and I hadn't had time to become the best buddies I'd envisioned, because her life was cut short, but I'd still felt bonded with her. I would miss her laugh and inviting grin. The more I thought about her, the more my determination rose to find out who, besides a client who wouldn't get off her back about retrieving his files from her, would kill someone so full of vitality.

The receiver was in my hand before I even realized my intentions. My fingers punched out the numbers for Ben's cell phone, numbers he'd given me less than an hour ago. Had it only been forty-five minutes since I'd been kissed into oblivion? And now I was scared back to the world. Why would someone call me with that cryptic message? Who had I scorned and what fury would visit me? Who the hell wanted to scare me like that?

Ben's cell rang and rang, and finally I got his voicemail. I left a quick message, something like call me back. I wasn't paying attention because my gaze had been drawn to the kitchen window, where a man-sized shadow passed across the pane of glass.

Chapter Eleven

I was pretty sure I whimpered but couldn't tell over the loud knocking of my heart in my chest. Who in the hell was outside my house?

The next question was where could I find a spur-of-the-moment weapon? This was a small town with little crime. Our police chief, though dressed as a knight in shining armor, had a paunch that could not go unnoticed; it had stretched his costume to the limit. And even if I took the time to call the police, would they get here before I was killed in slasher-movie style while running through the backyard with no weapon?

The kitchen was situated in the front of the house, and I'd turned off all the lights after seeing the shadow. I didn't want him to be able to track my progress through the house. I heard a creaking noise and realized it was the sound of footsteps on the front porch. *Oh, God, please keep me safe and help me find a damn weapon. Fast.*

I carefully pulled on the door to the walk-in pantry. My brain flashed back to my marathon cleaning session with the Bouquet. All the cleaning supplies were kept in the pantry, and I remembered Maggie pulling an old-style broom from there to sweep the floor. Once the door was open, with nary a squeak, I started feeling around in the dark, not wanting cans to fall or jars to rattle while my hand crept across the face of the wooden shelves.

Toward the back, on the left-hand side, I finally felt the long skinny handle of the broom. But when I tried to move it, it snagged on something close to the floor. I gave it a yank and it still stuck. I heard another squeaking sound from the front porch and feared I was running out of time. Shit. I'd have to find something else.

I thought about grabbing a jar of preserves or canned melon balls Aunt Gertie had left behind. I could either throw it at the intruder's head or use it as a club, but I was afraid the Mason jar's smooth sides would slip out of my hand at the moment I would need it most.

The only other solution that came to mind was to find some kind of bottled cleaner and spray it, and keep on spraying it until the bottle was empty. I was hoping for stinging eyes and limited vision for the guy. Then I could get away and call our most trusted law enforcement professionals, provided there was someone available when they had a murderer on the loose.

Sheesh. A murderer was on the loose. What if the person still creaking across my porch was the murderer, going after the women of the town, one by one?

I was truly starting to freak out. I'd gone from maybe someone trying to break in to potential murderer and hadn't called the cops before trying to defend myself with industrial-strength cleaner. But it was too late to back out now.

My heart was pounding so hard I was sure the neighbors, and the shadow outside, could hear it. I grabbed the first spray bottle I came in contact with and stopped on the other side of the pantry door. From this angle, I could make out the front door with its square stained-glass insert. The porch light was on, and it threw the figure standing on the porch in relief on my foyer rug.

I stayed in the kitchen, waiting for the person to make their next move. It had taken them long enough to get to the front door. Was this guy trying to give me a heart attack, too, along with the nervous tension?

And then the doorbell rang, which left me in a quandary. What kind of burglar, or murderer, or whatever, rings the doorbell before they take all your stuff and kill you? A serial Mary Kay sample leaver? If I answered the door, would the person shove it open and come in? Or if I didn't answer the door, would they figure I had left or was asleep and consider it an all-clear to come in and attack?

Screw the questions! Screw the anxiety! Even the stupid plastic bottle of whatever I'd grabbed was beginning to shake in my hand as anger surpassed the adrenaline coursing through my veins.

So I crept, quiet as a mouse, to the front door. Grasping the cool brass of the doorknob, I prayed for my life and that the spray bottle nozzle wouldn't be clogged. I yanked the door open like I was ready to kick some ass and take some names. I was shaking in my socks.

****

"What the hell is wrong with you?" I said as I paced the rag rug in the living room three minutes later. I had flipped on the lights for a better view of my prey. "I could have killed you. And for what? Nothing. You idiot."

"Killed me? Please, with your pitiful weapon?" Ben the Damned said in his deprecating voice.

I wanted to choke him almost as much as I wanted to jump him. He was sprawled on my floral couch, looking as yummy as ever. I was pissed and shaking and still that couldn't keep me from noticing the way his jeans accentuated all the very interesting parts of his body, like rock solid thighs and a bulge I was finding hard to ignore.

"With this spray bottle, you idiot, I could have blinded you for life. I would feel horrible, but you would have—"

He cut me off. "How exactly were you planning to blind me forever with a spray bottle of vegetable oil?"

"How...what...but..." I looked at the bottle in question, expecting to see Super Roach Killer or Spray So Clean. Instead, I saw a picture of a big tomato next to some carrots, with the words Vegetable Oil in bold red print beneath them. Cooking oil? *I* was the idiot. "Well maybe my plan was to coat you down and slide you out the door. Or...oh, just forget it. What were you doing out there?"

"I found your mask on the front seat of my truck and wanted to return it to you."

"You could have given it to me tomorrow when you brought back the Zorro costume." Unless he wanted to keep Zorro and put it on for me at a later date. Mmmm. No, no, no. I needed to not let my damn hormones overrule my better sense. Plus, he had nearly scared the life out of me. If nothing else, that should have killed some of the lust. But no, not me, perverse idiot that I was.

"That is true." He rubbed the shadow of stubble on his chin. "Would you go for 'I couldn't wait to see you again'?"

As if. "No, I would not go for that trite line. You saw me only an hour ago." I was mad and actually letting the object of my mad know it. That was some adrenaline.

Although, I was kind of melting under his smile and the romance of someone not being able to stay away from me. I mean, who wouldn't want some totally hot guy mooning over her?

Ahem.

"So, what are you really doing here?" I asked, tapping my sock-covered foot in my best imitation of the impatient temptress. Temptress, ha. I was still in my oldest sweatpants and a holey sweatshirt. How's that for tempting?

"Well, I really did want to see you again, but then as I pulled up at your house, my cell phone beeped with your message. I checked it from the car, and you sounded kind of scared, but distracted. And that's when I came up to the door."

"Oh, God, that's right. I forgot I was leaving you a voicemail when I saw the shadow at the kitchen window. Was that you going across the window?"

"No. I walked right up your pathway."

"But someone walked by the window. Are you sure it wasn't you?" I started pacing again. I wanted him to say it was him. Because if it wasn't Ben, then it had to be someone else, someone else who maybe had it in for yours truly. And I wasn't willing to think about that prospect right now.

"Like I said, I walked right up to the door. So I didn't walk in front of the window. And that means it must have been someone else." His voice deepened and his eyes—his green, green eyes—narrowed.

Apparently his protective instinct was going on high alert, because he got up from the couch and started pacing right along with me, but in the opposite direction. My living room was in no way big, and his cross-course pacing meant we kept wriggling around each other when our paths met. Which made for some interesting body part bumping. *Down, Ivy.*

"Did you get a good look at the person?" he asked, during one wriggle in the middle of the room that put his hip in direct contact with my lower stomach. Shivers ran down my spine, and not the spooked kind. My hands literally itched to grab him, so I folded them into fists and stuck them in the pockets of my sweats.

"Are you kidding me? I flipped off the lights as soon as I saw the shadow, and then you came to the door. Wait a minute, wait a minute. That means someone could still be lurking out in back of my house. Oh, no!"

Like a choreographed dance, we moved in tandem to shut off the two lights in the entryway and then came back to each other, whispering.

"Do you think he's still out there?" I asked.

"No, I'm pretty sure he's gone, with all the commotion we made. Actually, turning off the lights this late in the game was not our brightest idea. I doubt he's still here, and even if he is, I think we've probably let him know we know he's out there."

"Okay, the weird thing there is I understood that. And second, I, for one, am happy to let him know I'm aware he's out there, because it keeps him out of *here*."

"Point taken, but who do you think it was, and what did he or she want?"

"I don't know, but it's creepy. Everyone in town

must know I'm not exactly loaded, so it can't be theft." Even in my mind it sounded stupid to really think some person was going around killing all the women in the town, so I didn't offer that as an alternative to theft. Instead, I waited for him to come up with some bright idea and share it with me.

"I don't know what else it could be," he said. So much for bright ideas. "But it is very strange, coming so close on the heels of Janice's death earlier tonight. We haven't had a crime here in Martha's Point in years. Other than various rowdy brawls after too much drinking, and high school pranks, this is a quiet town. Then all of the sudden there's a death and a possible stalking."

I was spooked. My brain was not working right, with all the leftover adrenaline. There was a murderer on the loose, and let's not forget my lingerie thief. A creepy creeping person had been on my porch not long ago. I blamed all these things for the next words that came out of my mouth. "Very weird. You want to stay the night?"

Chapter Twelve

I retrieved fresh sheets and towels from the tiny linen closet in the hall for my guest. And wondered what on earth I thought I was doing by allowing (Allowing? Puh-lease. I'd *asked* him.) Ben Fallon to stay the night. Had I gone off the deep end?

He was temptation personified for me. And did I really, truly know that his story about not being the shadow was true? For that matter, how did I know he wasn't the killer?

Well, the last was a dumb question. Or was it? Ben had been with me, dancing and kissing, before I'd found Janice. But would he have had enough time to kill her while I was asking all those partygoers where I could find her? I didn't think so.

I decided to ask him. But maybe that would set him off, if he was the killer. Clean towels and a washcloth still clutched in my hand, I agonized over what to do. If he was the killer, I'd invited him into my house, and he was drinking beer from my refrigerator. If he wasn't, I could spend the night completely alone because I'd asked a stupid question. Argh.

All right, I'd think of something. But I really didn't see Ben as the killer. I put the towels and washcloth in the bathroom and went out to find him.

He was sitting on the couch again and looked relaxed. Too relaxed?

Misty Simon

"So, did you have a good time tonight, other than the whole murder thing?" Good one, Ivy, smooth, like Ben and Jerry's Chunky Monkey. Feeling the fool, I sat on the wing chair directly across from the couch.

"That was horrible," Ben said, his head hanging low. "I can't believe Janice is gone. We weren't really good friends or anything, she had moved here about a year ago, but she was nice the few times I met her. She did some of the ads for the newspaper, and she was always so easy to work with. I hope the police hustle and find out who killed her."

He sounded sincere, and my doubts were disappearing faster than the above-mentioned Chunky Monkey when I used the big spoon. I figured sometimes you had to trust your gut instinct, and though I didn't think I'd ever used mine, it was telling me to trust Ben. Or was that my libido talking?

"I'm not fully licensed yet on the private investigator thing, but I'm going to offer to help," he said, fierce determination glinting in his green eyes. "And even if they won't take my help, I may look into it myself."

"But what would you do?" I curled my legs up under me and pulled at a thread on the hem of my sweatpants, wishing I had something sexier to wear. But the frolicking bears on my pants and the hole in my shirt mocked me with their complete lack of sexual appeal. Maybe that was a good thing. I didn't want him to want me, right? Wrong, my body yelled. Okay, I wanted him to want me, but not before I knew him. Dammit, that was getting old.

He jerked me back to the conversation with his response. "I'd do my best to find out who killed her. I

102

know almost every person in town, and not many of them know I'm studying for a private investigator license. To them I'd be a concerned and nosy citizen. Someone might slip up and say something they didn't mean to let out when I'm around." He paused. "I know it's not a foolproof plan."

I must have done a rotten job concealing my skepticism. "I'm sorry," I said, feeling bad because I'd doubted his innocence and his ability to help. Who was I to tell someone they weren't good enough to help in some way? In fact, the whole helping thing was sounding more and more appealing. Maybe I could help too. I'd made up my mind earlier to find out who had killed someone so young and vibrant; perhaps this could be my opportunity. "I shouldn't have scoffed at you for wanting to help, Ben. You're better qualified than I am, and yet I'm trying to figure out a way to help, too. Forgive me?"

The sexy smile came back, and I had about two seconds to interpret it before Ben's lips were on mine again, which sent me spiraling out into the ether of fantasyland.

The shrill ringing of the telephone brought me back to earth and reminded me to tell Ben about the creepy voicemail message.

I ran to the kitchen and grabbed the phone off the wall. "Hello?" I said, seriously afraid it would be the deep-voiced creepy caller again.

"Ivy, I'm so glad you're there," Bella's words tumbled one over another. "I'm assuming you got home safe since you answered the phone. Can you believe what happened tonight? I don't think we've had a murder here in about ten years. I'm going to come over.

It's too spooky in my house right now. If I'm not there in ten minutes, come looking for me." And she hung up.

Okay, I'd had no time to tell her anything, and now I had to explain to Ben that we would be having another guest. So much for more kissing, although maybe the presence of another person would keep me out of trouble. At least I could hope. I replaced the phone in its cradle in the kitchen and turned to face a smiling Ben.

"So where did we leave off? I think this hand was here." He touched the sensitive skin behind my ear, effectively cradling my head. "And my other hand was here." He rested his other hand on the swell of my hip. "And my lips were definitely..." And he kissed me again.

His mouth caressed mine, sending tingles down my back and turning my legs to goo. His grip on my hip tightened and kept me upright as he eased my lips apart, then plundered with his tongue. My head was swimming and parts of me were definitely liquefying.

And then the doorbell rang.

"Shit," I said, breaking away from those soft lips.

"Busy night around here."

"Yeah, lucky me."

"Do you want me to go?"

Decision time. I could tell him yes, since Bella would be here and between the two of us we could probably protect ourselves. But then again, on the other hand, why should I send Ben out into the night? It wasn't like I didn't have the room, and I would rather have a guy here, too. Not discounting the fact that the thought of Ben spending the night in my house with me right down the hall was very appealing. Maybe I could sneak out in the middle of the night...

I put the brakes on that thought. I needed to sort out the hormones from the real feelings first. How much of a factor was lust? And how much was it my heart telling me Ben was a really great guy I could see my new self having more than a fling with? Argh!

"No, don't leave. It's only Bella; I guess she's spending the night, too. Do you mind?" I walked toward the front door with its stained glass window.

"Hmmm. Decisions, decisions. Two beautiful women, one me, a little house with cozy furniture. I think I can deal."

He followed me to the door, and I socked him in the arm for his insolence. "Shut up."

I flipped the lock on the door, and it flung open with the force of a hurricane. Bella, two suitcases, a duffle bag, and a plastic grocery sack came flying through the door and went straight into the kitchen. "Hello, Ivy. Ben." There was the crinkling of plastic in the kitchen as I watched her take out dip, chips, and a bottle of wine and put them on the counter.

And then she did a classic double-take. "Ben? Oh my, my, my. Am I interrupting something?" The smug smile said she didn't care, and was truly enjoying the moment as well as my discomfort.

"No, you're not interrupting anything." I hoped I wasn't sporting a completely embarrassing blush. "Ben's staying the night because I'm spooked about the murder thing, too. But I have plenty of covers, and you both can stay." I bit my lip and plunged into the next part. "Since you're both here right now, I forgot to tell you about a scary voicemail I got when I checked my messages after Ben left."

"What? What message?" Ben asked, a frown wrinkling his forehead.

"Let me play it, and then I'll answer any questions you have." I dialed the voice mail service number and played the message for them. When it was over, goose bumps popped out on my arms.

Ben asked to hear it again. He started taking some notes in one of those little memo books we all had as kids. "So you didn't recognize the voice?" he said, looking all serious and extremely hot.

His hands rested on his rock solid thighs, his expression intense, but my eyes kept wandering to the package I'd accidentally fondled at the bar and was thinking of on-purpose fondling again, sometime very soon. *Down girl, your hormones are sparking so hard you're liable to burn the freaking house down.*

"Uh." Man alive, it was hot in here. "No. I didn't recognize the voice."

"Well, the message was pretty cryptic. You did a good job by keeping it. Now we have to figure out what it means."

Bella went back to the kitchen to get some tortilla chips and guacamole. I'd turned her on to the Mexican snack the first night we'd gotten together, and now she was addicted, like me.

Ben took the opportunity to sit on the arm of my chair and toy with the ends of my hair. "Did I tell you how much I love your hair?" he asked right next to my ear. "And this spot right here, under your ear, is so sexy. As soon as I get near you, it's like a homing beacon leading me right to the spot and the scent there."

Holy God, help me. Was it possible to have an

auditory orgasm? If so, let me tell you it was mind shattering. I was pretty surprised I didn't slide right out of the chair and onto the floor.

Bella came waltzing back into the living room, loaded with goodies, and was a welcome distraction from my weak will when it came to Ben Fallon. "All right, lady and gent, here's chips, guac, and your choice of wine or Corona beer. Let's dig in and try to figure out what the hell is going on in our sleepy town."

Unfortunately, we got a little drunk (read: we all passed out in my living room) talking about Ben and Bella as kids and teenagers. Mostly we were trying to distract ourselves after we realized how little information we really had about what was happening in Martha's Point. I got all the dirt, but when I woke up in the morning, sprawled in my wingback chair, I felt like that dirt was lodged in my mouth.

"Yeck," I said, and got a groan in return. Was it a masculine Ben groan? I looked down over the side of the fabric chair to see Ben lying on the floor, using one of my boots from the entryway as a pillow. No way was that comfortable, but he looked so cute.

I almost gave in to the desire to kiss him awake, then pulled back, horrified, when I thought of what my breath must smell like the morning after.

In my whole sheltered life, I'd never over-indulged before, and now I knew why. My head hurt worse than it did when I had nagging customers on a premenstrual day, and my body was suffering from the uncomfortable chair I'd slept in. Ack!

I was mentally reviewing the meager contents of my refrigerator in hopes of some bright inspiration for a post-binge breakfast when the antique clock on the mantel started sounding out the hour.

"Oh, no." I didn't think I wanted to see what time it was. The sun was shining in through the living room window, which meant it was definitely some time after seven in the morning. The ding, ding, ding continued, and even my fuddled mind could count to ten, which was when the dinging stopped. I looked to the mantel for confirmation and almost had a coronary.

It was ten a.m. *TEN A.M.?* I was so screwed. The shop was supposed to open in exactly thirty minutes, and here I was, still in my sweatpants and sweatshirt from last night. Not to mention my mouth felt horrid, my hair was probably a mess, and there were two people sleeping in my living room, dead to the world.

Yep, I was so screwed.

"All right, people. Up, up, up." I clapped my hands like I was at some kind of elementary school assembly, but it did the job. A bleary-eyed Bella peeked over the back of the couch at me, and Ben sat up from the floor with a snap.

"Wha..." Bella said, and Ben groaned. Okay, that was definitely the groan I'd heard earlier, and it was still as yummy as it had been then.

"I need you guys to get up. I have to be at the shop in twenty minutes, which means you have fifteen minutes to grab your stuff."

Ben had this terrible sleep indentation on his cheek in the form of the stitchwork on my boot. I snickered. He was so damn cute.

"Leave the key, Ivy, and we'll lock up after ourselves," Bella said.

Was I comfortable with doing that? I mean, Bella was my friend, but I'd only met her a handful of days ago. And if Ben and I got to know each other better, he could end up being my lover, but this was my house, and I'd never had anything that was solely mine before. Was I ready to blithely hand over the keys?

"Don't think so hard, for God's sake. You're giving me a headache just looking at you," Bella said, as Ben fell over and started snoring.

"I'm not thinking too hard. I'm, uh, trying to think about how that would work. Besides, don't you have to go to work today?"

"It will work in the way that I will bring the key to you before I go to work, which, if you remember correctly, is right down the street from The Masked Shoppe." She pulled a pillow over her head, dismissing me.

"You don't have to be so bitchy," I said, but under my breath.

"I heard that, and yes, I do. I'm hung over and tired, which makes me bitchy. And you're trying to kick me out of this very comfy couch at the crack of dawn so you can be all obsessive-compulsive about your shop. Who cares?"

I saw the opportunity to cull a little of the wind from her sails and couldn't resist it. "If by the crack of dawn you mean ten in the morning, then I apologize."

That got her moving. She shot off the couch like someone had lit a firecracker under her rear end. "Shit. Ten in the morning? I scheduled a special appointment today at eleven, and I'm still in my clothes from last night. I'm so screwed."

"Funny, but I was thinking the same thing when I tried to get your ass moving ten minutes ago."

"Yeah, yeah, whatever. Come on, loverboy," she

said, pressing a socked foot into Ben's belly. "Get up. We have to go. You might not have anything that needs to be done today, but we do, and you can't stay."

Another grunt came from the floor, and Ben, absolutely adorable with his rumpled brown hair and sleepy green eyes, sat up again. "Oh, man, I feel like I spent the night on my old bed at my Grandma's house." He stretched his awesome arms and broad shoulders, making my mouth water. I was going to have a tough time staying celibate if he kept moving that way. I was starting to think my whole mind-over-lust approach was way outdated.

"That must have been some bed your grandma saved for you, because you spent the night on Ivy's wood floor with a boot for a pillow. Nice sleep creases, by the way." Bella moved toward my bedroom and its attached bathroom with a lot more purpose than I would have given her credit for five minutes ago. Thirty seconds later the water started running. Which left me alone with Ben.

And for once he looked sheepish. Where was the confident, ballsy guy who didn't care about anything or the way it made him look? Oh, jeez, another facet found.

Rising slowly to his feet, Ben gave me a lopsided smile and cupped my chin, leaning down to place a soft kiss on my forehead before heading in the direction of the second bathroom. "Morning," he called over his shoulder.

"And what, pray tell, was that, Miss Ivy?" From the looks of her, Bella was done in the bathroom, and as usual was stunning even after sleeping on a couch.

"I am not at all sure, Miss Bella, but I've never

been so turned on by a mere brushing of lips over my forehead. Not even when I had a major crush on the next-door neighbor boy and he touched my forehead to check for fever during babysitting duty."

"That's a little sick, Ivy. Haven't you had any hot moments in your life since a babysitter?"

"The answer to that question is 'not really,' and you had to be there."

Chapter Thirteen

As I walked the short distance to The Masked Shoppe, I fervently prayed everyone was as exhausted as I was after the long night and would not be waiting in front of the store to return their costumes. It was Sunday, after all, and the shop would stay open until seven tonight to accommodate everyone.

Of course my life did not run in that kind of nice logical line. So, instead of the empty stoop I was hoping for, I came upon a crowd of people. In the center of that crowd was Kitty, and she, of course, was talking.

"Well, folks, really, I expect Ivy at any moment. I know she'll remember to come and open the store for all of you. Surely she didn't get so drunk last night she would forget everyone was bringing back their costumes today. I wish I could do it for her, but she's the boss and has the only key."

I couldn't decide whether to call her a dirty name or throw her out in the street and tell her never to darken my frickin' door again. I absolutely did not need this right now.

But the old Ivy rose from deep inside and I kept my mouth shut. It was better to smile and get the job done instead of calling Kitty out before I even had a decent cup of coffee.

I made a production of looking at the sign on the door and then at the watch on my wrist. "Hi folks, sorry

I'm on time." That got a laugh from a couple of people, though not from Kitty, who quickly transformed her scowl into the pleasant smile I was used to seeing on her narrow face. I'd always thought it was fake, and now I knew she could whip it out anytime she wanted to and it would look the same as when she genuinely smiled. If she'd ever actually genuinely smiled.

The whole group of people trailed in after me and formed a line in front of the counter. I was thankful I hadn't taken a chunk out of Kitty earlier. How on earth would I have survived this on my own? Also, a lot of the customers still only went to Kitty. I might have been anonymous last night and so everyone was nice to me, but in the cold light of morning, without my mask and flapper costume, it was business as usual, and that included several very dirty looks. It seemed people were not soon going to welcome me into their little town as I'd originally thought. I guess between being from California and the grumblings from locals that I didn't deserve the shop since I'd never come to visit my aunt (Bella's information), I continued as persona non grata. I still hoped that would change but was getting the distinct feeling I was tilting at windmills.

Two hours and about sixty costumes later, I wasn't sure how I had even survived *with* the help. We'd checked in so many costumes they were a blur of fur and masks and cloth. But, I thought, when I checked the sales for this, our busiest season, I would be pleasantly surprised by the amount of money we had pulled in.

The bell rang and another customer walked in, this one with a pair of jet-black silk pants and a two-toned cape. He also had a genie costume in vibrant purple. I pulled Mr. Jorgensen's receipt from the box on the counter and checked his rental agreement against his return. "Looks like everything is here, sir. Thank you to you and Doris for renting from us. If you could sign the bottom of the receipt, here at the X, you can be on your way."

Mr. Jorgensen was a farmer from the outskirts of town, and a wonderfully funny guy. He and his wife were in their fifties, and Doris sometimes came in to take advantage of my little back room.

"Thank you, Ivy. The party was a good time until that poor woman was found. Did you hear any more about what happened?" His big hand held my pumpkin-topped pen like it was a fragile piece of china as he scrawled his signature across the bottom of the page.

"Actually, that's what almost everyone has been asking today. I don't know anything more than what we saw last night."

"Yep, I hear the police force is keeping things pretty close to the vest. We haven't had a murder in Martha's Point in about ten years, and it has sure shook up the people around here. Did you hear how she died?"

"Can't say that I have, Mr. Jorgensen. You?" I couldn't tell him I was actually the one who had found her. I'd been asked to keep the information close to my own vest, or rather the kicking jade green shirt I'd put on this morning, one of Bella's hand-me-downs.

"Nope. But I did hear they found blood on her top from a stab wound. They figure that's what got her." Tidbit passed on to the next grape on the vine, he left with a backhanded wave.

I put Mr. Jorgensen's costume on the rack behind the counter. Kitty stood next to me, helping another costumer, and I felt bone tired all of a sudden. She could handle things for a few moments. There was only one other person in line, and no one else in the shop.

"I'm going to take some of these costumes to the back, Kitty. Holler if you need me."

"Oh, I'll be fine, Ivy. Nothing I can't handle on my own. You run along and have your break, and I'll stay right here."

Take a deep breath and let it roll off your back, I counseled myself. I thought maybe I was too sensitive to her and this only proved it further. I needed to stop listening to her, and I also needed to remember who the owner was—me. No amount of her mouth was going to change that.

So, ignoring Kitty and her catty attitude, I took the six outfits from the rack behind us, including Mr. Jorgensen's recent returns, and walked into the back room. I sat down and spread the garments out before me. The genie costume and the pirate were in perfect condition. A little stitching on the hem would fix the princess outfit. Some kind of oil spotted the pumpkin costume, from the looks of the shiny spots on the green satin leaves around the throat. The werewolf looked okay, if a little matted. And the black pants from Mr. Jorgensen would need dry cleaning, as all the fabric outfits did.

Then I picked up the cape. It was silky black on the outside and had a deep red lining. I inspected it as I did all the other costumes and almost missed the fist-sized stain on the tall collar. It was dry, and a deeper color than the red lining. It wasn't greasy like the oil, or fruity smelling like the wine stain I'd found on another cape earlier. This stain was like a splatter of paint, but crusty. In fact, the only thing I'd ever seen like it was when I pricked my finger with a needle trying to fix a sleeve on one of the costumes and ended up bleeding on the damn thing.

The thought stopped me cold. Blood? The image of Janice, dead in a back room of the Barn, jumped into my head, and I remembered the blood I'd seen coating Janice's chest. I shuddered as I remembered Mr. Jorgensen's comment about the blood on her body.

A scary idea entered my head and I wondered what exactly I was thinking by even entertaining it for more than a single moment. Mr. Jorgensen couldn't have killed Janice, could he? I had no idea if they even knew each other. And why would he have mentioned the blood if he was the one who had killed her and in the process had splattered some blood on his collar?

He was an honest and good farmer, from what I'd heard and seen for myself, and I knew he wasn't dumb. When he came in, he always talked with me and he seemed so nice. Could it be possible he was capable of murder? Then again, maybe my imagination was going wild and this wasn't really blood. Or was it?

Chapter Fourteen

I couldn't get the stain out of my mind the rest of the night. It could have been juice or punch, but when I'd scraped at the edges, rust-colored flecks came off. I'd never seen juice crust like that.

It was freaky, and I wasn't even going to try to handle this one on my own. So, first thing in the morning, I called the knight in shining armor...er, the sheriff, but got put right into his voicemail. O-kay.

"Hi, this is Ivy Morris from The Masked Shoppe. I, ah, well, during my costume returns yesterday, I found one that you might be interested in seeing. I'll hold onto it until I hear from you." I left my number and prayed I was wrong. I really liked Mr. Jorgensen.

An hour later, after washing yesterday's dishes and cleaning up after the impromptu party from Saturday night with Bella and Ben, I decided to go to work. Surely the sheriff could figure out I was at the store if I didn't answer the phone at the house.

So I found myself behind the counter when the police came charging into the shop like I'd stolen the last doughnut at Mad Martha's Milk and Munchies.

"Ivy Morris?" The tall, older guy before me looked a lot different without his costume.

"Yes, I'm Ivy."

"We're here regarding your message. We rushed over as soon as we heard it. Do you have an office we can meet in to discuss this issue?"

Well, that was certainly vague enough. I turned the store over to Kitty, who had shown up thirty minutes ago, and took the two officers back to the little cubbyhole I called an office. The embarrassing thing was I didn't have enough chairs to seat my company. The office was only big enough for a desk, a bookshelf and one chair.

"I'm sorry about the limited space," I said, feeling about two inches high. What kind of business only has one office and room for only one chair in it? Something else I'd need to work on. Yay.

"All we're interested in is the costume, Ms. Morris. We don't need to get comfortable here, but thank you for your concern."

He wasn't so bad after all.

"Well, Officer..." I left the title hang.

"Now I'm the one who is sorry, Ms. Morris. I got ahead of myself. I'm Detective Jameson, and this is my partner, Detective Bartley." An attractive woman wearing a great smoke-gray suit nodded her auburn head in my direction but remained silent. "Now that the introductions are out of the way, can we see this costume?"

"Absolutely, Detective Jameson. If you'll, um..." I gestured with my hand to get him to inch his way to the left so I could access the little closet on the wall. God, how mortifying. We scootched around each other and did this kind of funky two-step so I could get around him and open the door. I pulled the cape from the shallow enclosure and handed it over.

"This is the costume. A gentleman brought it in last night, right before we closed, and I saw the stain. I figured it was punch or something and didn't think much about it until I scraped at the stain and rust-colored flakes started coming off. I stopped right then and put it away to think about overnight. I didn't want to do anything to ruin evidence, if that's what it is. I hope I did the right thing?" Damn, there was the stupid lilt at the end of a sentence again. It drove me nuts and made me feel like a child looking for approval. Where was the brazen woman from Saturday? Truthfully, I think she took a hike when Janice died.

The officers thanked me and left with the cape in a plastic bag with the store logo on it. Two seconds after I came back to the counter, Kitty was on me like a starving dog with a tasty chicken leg to gnaw on.

"What were Tom and Debbie doing here?"

It took me a moment to connect the names with the two detectives. When I did, I thought the name Debbie so did not fit the queen of fashion who had stood silently in my office with her bright red hair.

I hesitated, not sure what exactly I wanted to say to Kitty. She'd been giving me weird looks since she'd shown up this morning, like I shouldn't be here and yet I was. Actually the looks had started Saturday night when I saw her standing across the crowd from me over Janice's body. I didn't know what the deal was, but I had more important things to think about, things that had nothing to do with Kitty.

"Well, the detectives were here to ask me a few questions because I was at the Barn that night."

"Hmmph, they didn't have any questions for me," she said, and I hoped she'd drop it there. Of course, that had never worked for me before. "I wonder what they wanted from you. Did you ask anything specific? They said something about a message you left them."

Shit! "Ah, that was about a, ah, piece of paper I found in one of the costumes that came in yesterday."

"Really, a piece of paper? What did it say?"

I was totally in a huge, dark, deep hole of my own making and had no idea how to get back out. And then the phone rang. *Thank you, Alexander Graham Bell!*

"Why don't you get that, Kitty? I have a few things to do in the back, and then I have an errand to run. Do you think you can handle things for a little bit?"

She nodded as she picked up the phone, and I breathed a sigh of relief.

I wasted no time hustling into the boudoir section to unpack the new shipment of plus-sized lingerie I'd ordered to replace my dwindling supply. My little back room was certainly popular, and fortunately no one had stolen anything else.

While I cut tape and unwrapped the plastic packets of bras and panties, my mind wandered into Ben territory. He hadn't been at the house when I came home from work yesterday, not that I expected him to be, after I'd kicked him out. But he'd left me a message that he would be on my doorstep this evening, waiting to take me out to dinner. Yes, he'd called and moved the date up from Thursday to tonight. *Woo-hoo!*

But then I had an attack of conscience. Should I be pursuing a relationship when my friend was dead? Was it uncouth (ooh, good word) of me to be trying to get into something with Ben when I'd vowed to find a killer? I didn't have any good answers, so I called him back and told him no three times, and yet I was going out tonight. I couldn't for the life of me figure out how he did it. Perhaps it was his powers of persuasion.

Perhaps it was some odd form of over-the-phone hypnotism. More than likely, it was the fact I really didn't mean any of my previous "no's" and got tired of making him play the game.

As I opened another box, a beautiful set of black lace panties and matching bra caught my eye. I still hadn't decided what to wear tonight, as I had no idea where we were actually going. But that didn't mean I couldn't pick out something to satisfy my inner need to feel at least a little sexy.

Picking out an outfit for tonight wasn't actually going to be hard, since Bella had confiscated all my brown outfits and I now had about ten items hanging in my closet to mix and match. Not a spot of brown in any of them. The one brown thing I still owned I'd hidden from Bella and her kamikaze approach to emptying my armoire. It was the outfit I'd been complimented on at my last job. I couldn't let her get rid of it.

I walked over to the beautiful antique sideboard I'd moved into the boudoir last week to house some of the more risqué items we carried. I found out through talking with customers that nothing turned some women off from buying a beautiful and flowing nightgown in satin as fast as a life-sized vibrator for the lonely (or playful). But I used the top of the cabinet as a display area and draped a short baby-doll lace concoction over the ornate molding lining the back.

Really, I was becoming more comfortable with the items we sold. I had even installed a buzzer and a separate cash register (modern, this time, so I could operate it without assistance) in the back so people could feel less conspicuous when purchasing their items. When a customer was ready to buy one of our "novelty" items, they pushed the buzzer, which sounded up at the front counter, and I would come back to process the transaction. It worked out nicely.

And I was thankful the new lingerie had come in. I'd placed an order with our online supply company, Sass and Lace, for rush delivery. They only sold to retail stores and were very gracious in getting the order to me as soon as possible. Phew!

I looked at the slim watch on my wrist and almost jumped out of my skin. The day had flown by, and I still needed to run my errand. I hightailed it out of the shop with a backhanded wave for Kitty, and hit the street running, in a very sedate and dignified way, of course. It wouldn't do for a proprietress to run like a hellion down the street where every current and potential customer could see her. But I needed to get to Bella quickly because she was doing my hair and nails for tonight.

When I walked in the door to her shop, there was no ringing bell, and I envied her. What it must be like to not have to listen to an annoying bell all day. Bella was ready for me and led me right to a purple-cushioned chair.

"Sooooo. Hot date tonight?" she asked.

"No, not a hot date. Ben and I are simply going out for dinner."

"So, hot date. Come on, Ivy, get into the mood a little better. If I were going out with Ben, it would definitely be a hot date."

"Why don't you go out with Ben?" I asked, truly curious. "I mean, you guys know each other, and you're both intelligent, attractive, single people. What's the deal?"

"Puh-lease. Ben and I go way back, yes, but we know each other too well. Haven't you ever had a male friend you were totally non-sexual with? I can't even think of Ben and sex in the same sentence. Now you and Ben and sex I could probably wrap my mind around, though I wouldn't really want any details."

"Ha, ha. You are a fountain of information."

"You want information? I'll give you information," she said, draping me with a slate-gray cape. "One time Ben decided it would be a good idea to do one of those ding-dong-ditch things where you ring someone's doorbell and leave a flaming paper bag of dog poo on the doorstep for them. They're supposed to see the fire and stamp it out with their shoe and in the process get dog crap on themselves and any other place within a few feet of the bag. Well, it's an oldie but a goodie, and Ben wanted to try it on our homeroom teacher in eighth grade." She paused to move around some things on the counter behind her. "He gets everything ready and scoops the poop, puts it in the bag, snakes a lighter from his mom, and goes to Mr. Seaver's house."

She snipped some hair from behind my left shoulder and I watched her in the mirror, waiting for the punch line for what I assumed was going to be a snort-worthy story.

"Everything is ready," she continued. "He lights the bag, rings the doorbell, and starts to run from the door. Problem is, the bag ripped at some point and most of the poop, which he made sure was soft and fresh, is on the sidewalk. He steps right into it, slips, and falls on his ass in the pile of crap. He didn't get up fast enough because he didn't want to get any more dog crap on his clothes, he said. And that's how Mr. Seaver caught him lying on the sidewalk covered in crap. Let me tell you, Ben was in detention every afternoon for the rest of the year, and the teacher made him clean every smudge of dog doo from the porch and sidewalk with a toothbrush."

Imagining Ben down on his knees with his little toothbrush, I snorted until my sides hurt. Once I got myself under control, Bella proceeded to tell me stories about Ben and his various childhood screw-ups, (including one very funny tale about a dog, a bush, and hiding from an overly friendly girl) and his return to Martha's Point after college.

I was still laughing thirty minutes later when Bella made me close my eyes while she whipped me around in the chair to face the mirror. "Voila!"

I opened my eyes, still a little dizzy from the spin, and gasped in surprise. I was...I was beautiful.

I almost started crying until Bella threatened me with her shears. "I know I was only going to do your hair and nails, but I'm glad you let me do the whole thing. You look fabulous."

And I did. My hair was soft and shiny, touchable. The makeup was subtle but emphasized my eyes and cheekbones enough to make my face look thinner, and in addition my lashes looked a mile long. Very nice. Now I had to come up with an outfit that did the face and hair justice.

I jumped up, gave Bella a huge hug, and laughed as she wished me luck tonight. I didn't need luck. I was fabulous.

I hustled back to the shop, locked up after Kitty, and headed for home. I'd left a light on for myself, and the soft glow from my front room welcomed me. I absolutely loved this house and the grounds around it. Every time I approached the cottage, I silently thanked Great-Aunt Gertie. Not for dying, of course, but for leaving me this beautiful piece of heaven, and my shop.

I had a viable income, a roof over my head, and now I guessed I was approaching a place where a relationship could be my next step. But I didn't want to get ahead of myself. A lot of Bella's stories had been about Ben with roughly half the population of Martha's Point. Did I really want to get involved with someone like that?

I didn't know and, until I was sure, I was going to be cautious. Or so I told myself until the doorbell rang an hour later and I opened the door to the sexiest man I had seen outside of a magazine or movie in, well, really, forever.

Ben stood on the porch, his green eyes twinkling and a smile on his face. He'd tucked his white oxford shirt into a pair of chinos that fell at precisely the right place on his brown suede shoes. Unlike his previous outfits, this shirt looked freshly ironed. His hair was damp, which sent my imagination into overdrive with shower scenes, naked bodies, and fresh clean skin.

Get a grip! I silently berated myself as I figuratively wiped the drool from my mouth. When I finally remembered my manners, I invited him in for a pre-dinner drink, and he produced a handful of daisies from behind his back.

Okay, this was getting to be too much. Not only was he totally yummy, but he'd also brought flowers? I wasn't so sure this was merely dinner any more. This felt like, for lack of a better word, courting.

Chapter Fifteen

One car ride later, I was almost positive it was courting. He helped me out of the car before I even had a chance to open the door, and offered his arm as we walked the short distance from the parking lot. An old Victorian house converted into three dining rooms and the kitchen, the restaurant was in a part of town I had yet to explore. A path wound its way from the parking lot to massive oak double-front doors. Soft light filtered out through the beveled panes of glass fitted into the top of each one.

Was I ready for courting? I mean, Ben was certainly hot and funny and nice. But I was still attempting to nail down the proprietress thing and trying to figure out who stole my underwear, plus ferreting out who would want to kill Janice. Did I have time for a relationship on top of everything else?

The answer was not fast in coming. Ben held the left door open and ushered me into the vestibule with his hand on the small of my back, which sent a little tingle of pleasure racing up my spine.

A sharply dressed man stood at a podium, looking officious. "Two for Fallon," Ben said to him, and my mind started playing that ridiculous game where you imagine yourself with the guy's last name. Complete with curlicues and hearts. Mrs. Ivy Fallon. Had a nice ring to it.

No! I jerked myself out of Inappropriate Fantasyland as we were led to a table draped in white linen and topped with two slender candlesticks in a shade of red that reminded me of blood. The color brought back thoughts of Janice's murder and dampened my enthusiasm for dinner. The police had to have some leads. Why did I think they needed my help when they had training and expertise of their own?

Maybe because I had more invested in finding out who had cut down my friend in the prime of her life. Sure, the police would do their jobs, but they had other cases, too, and two heads were always better than one. The metaphor was a little off, but the purpose was there.

"So what'll you have?" Ben said, breaking into my morose thoughts.

I shook my head to clear it of murder and mayhem and reached for a menu, which when opened showed no prices. I was freaked out now, but for an entirely different reason. What kind of small town reporter, excuse me, food critic, could afford to take a first date to a restaurant without prices in the menu?

Please don't let me be bankrupting him, I thought as I ordered the least-expensive-looking thing—the chicken fettuccine alfredo. Ben ordered some duck à la something, and wine was brought to the table.

After over-indulging this last weekend, I didn't even want to look at alcohol, much less participate in its consumption. I declined, my hand over my glass, and Ben poured for himself.

"So, well, this is nice," I said. *Dumb, Ivy, dumb.*

"Yeah, I like it. Jerry makes a wicked chicken fettuccine. I think you'll be pleased."

"Jerry?"

"The chef," he said, as a breeze streamed past me and in its wake left a man who could have doubled as a Sumo wrestler. I couldn't see any of the other diners past his girth and wondered if this was the infamous Jerry. The single-breasted chef jacket and tall white hat could have had something to do with my clever deduction.

"Jerry," Ben said. Suspicion confirmed. "This is Ivy Morris. Ivy, Jerry Bourcheron."

I extended my hand for a firm and business-like shake (after all, Jerry might need a costume one day, though I didn't know what I had that would fit him), and I was neatly yanked out of my chair into a hug that would have crushed a lesser woman.

"I love a woman with some meat on her bones," Jerry said, and I struggled for a moment not to take that as an insult. "You, bella mia, are in for a treat. I am pulling out all the stops for my friend Ben tonight, and you will be treated to the finest meal in the history of meals." He finally released me, and I filled my lungs with air as he kissed my hand and stomped off. He reminded me of the Jolly Green Giant except he was dressed in white.

"You have to love Jerry," Ben said with a little smirk on his face, giving me the impression he knew something I didn't and was enjoying the moment.

"He's very friendly," I said in my most diplomatic tone.

Ben laughed, the belly laugh that made my insides liquefy. I waited for the hilarity to stop before I said, "Stuff it, Ben." Bella would not be proud of my comeback, as it was extremely childish, but I gave myself points for saying anything at all.

A waiter came over, bearing a basket of bread and a small dish into which he poured extra virgin-looking olive oil and used one of those cool pepper-grinder things to complete a dip for the French bread. Ben sat back and gave me his full-on smile with the dimples and all. I started to feel distinctly itchy.

"So, Ivy Morris. I have finally managed to get you all to myself and now can begin my nefarious plan."

"Good word," I said, before I could stop myself, and then endured the blush I knew was creeping up my neck.

"You like that one?" Ben said.

"Uh, no. I was, er, enjoying the bread." I plastered a fake smile over my red flaming face and prayed my babbling would distract him enough for us to have a normal conversation.

"Really. Well, me, I like big words. I think they're fascinating. Don't you, Ivy? They are so interesting when you try to put them into a sentence."

This was a very odd conversation. In all the time I'd known Ben, which admittedly was not very long, I had never heard him try to use big words. I mean, this would have seriously tipped the scale toward jumping his bones immediately. Some women fall for a tight behind. Me? I fall for a silver tongue. Hmmm, that didn't sound right, but it did sound intriguing. Either way, it seemed something was fishy in Denmark.

"You find words fascinating?" I asked. Come on, Ivy, the man was a journalist after all. Why wouldn't he find words fascinating?

"Oh, yes. Absolutely splendiferous. I try and expand my mind every day, dipping into the dictionary and testing my dauntlessness and, ah, endeavoring to make myself more learned."

Now this might have flown—have I mentioned big words coming out of Ben's mouth had made my thighs start tingling? Right. This might have flown if I hadn't seen Ben's eyes dart over and down to where I thought his left hand was. I heard the flutter of pages before he said "endeavoring." Did the man have a freaking dictionary right now? And if he did, how could I expose him without getting caught or being overt?

In the end, as Ben continued to spew words that would win you top points in Scrabble, I dropped my napkin on the floor. Hokey, I know, but what else could I have done? I bent over to retrieve it and a waiter was already there picking it up. "Leave it," I hissed, startling the boy, who couldn't have been more than sixteen. We had a brief tug-of-war, and I won. Score one for the bigger-boned woman. I can take on a scrawny teenager in the blink of an eye.

By this time, Ben was starting to get to his feet, and I popped up from beneath the table. During the tussle for the napkin, I'd had enough time to catch Ben with a copy of *Roget's 21st Century Thesaurus*. I wasn't far off when I'd thought dictionary. Ah-ha. So the question now begging to be answered: Was he mocking me or flirting with me? And if he was flirting, how did he know big words were my thing? We would soon see.

"So, big words," I said, as I straightened the tablecloth on the table and resumed eating the bread dipped in oil and pepper. Delicious, delicious carbs.

"Um, yeah, big words. Love 'em."

"Funny you should say that. My family and I are always trying to one-up each other with big words.

How about you? Do you use them to say, spiff up your writing?"

"Yes, yes, of course, spiff up my work."

"So what great word have you come up with to use for your next article? Vociferous? Mastication? Asininity?" I heard the whir of pages and decided to take pity on him. "What's going on, Ben? Why did you bring a thesaurus to dinner?"

For the first time in our acquaintance it was actually Ben who looked a little pink under the collar. "Man, she's going to hate me," he said under his breath, but I still heard it.

"I'm not going to hate you."

"Not you. Bella."

"What's she got to do with this?" And then it dawned on me. Bella had asked about the big-word thing once, and I had told her all about the word championships and the notes my family and I would slip each other trying to stump someone. (For instance: What's another word for 'mendicant'?) That little snot must have told Ben so he could impress me. Though why he had to try to impress me was beyond my comprehension.

"I asked her if you had any interests, and she came out with 'big words.' I thought I'd give it a shot, but I guess I messed it up. I shouldn't have brought this damn thesaurus."

"What was your first clue?" I asked, and then giggled until he joined in. His masculine laugh threatened to turn my knees to mud. Thank God I was already sitting down.

I think for the first time I really believed Ben was interested me as a person. He certainly went to enough trouble to find out what my likes were, although Bella might need to be seriously maimed for leaking my secrets.

Dinner flew by as course after course arrived at our table. Following the lobster bisque soup, my chicken fettuccine alfredo arrived. By the time it was set on the table, I already felt like I'd swallowed a whale.

I looked at Ben as he started cutting his duck whatever. His eyes widened as he really took in the portion before him, and I said, "Well, that certainly is ambitious of you."

"I was thinking the same thing." He lifted a forkful of duck to his mouth. "I've never eaten so much food in my life. I may have to risk the wrath of Jerry and ask for a doggy bag."

"There is no way they call leftovers doggy bags here."

"Absolutely. What else would you call it? This is rural Virginia. We have doggy bags. Why, is it called something else in posh Southern California?"

"Did you know 'posh' actually stands for Port Over Starboard Home? It originated when wealthy people took ocean liners and ships across the Atlantic, and meant the cabin view they preferred." Ben looked at me with a gleam in his eye and I went back to the subject at hand. Doggy bags—fascinating. "No, it's not different in California. I...well, I just can't see Jerry handing out bags with little doggy logos on them for his food."

"Just you wait," Ben said, but I barely heard him because a scene broke out three tables away from us.

"You damn well *will* give me those files," a man said, his voice loud and his face bright red. "I will *not* wait for some asshole attorney to muck up things while my project goes unprinted." He leaned in toward his dinner companion, menace in his every move. "I don't care if she's been dead three years or three days. You're out of your mind if you think I'll wait another two months. Get me the files or prepare for a court battle." At the end, he'd started yelling. Everyone in the restaurant heard him, but most pretended to mind their own business. A few shot evil looks at him as he threw his linen napkin on the table and stalked around the other tables to the door, which he slammed behind him in a dramatic exit.

"I wonder what that was all about," I said, continuing to watch the older gentleman left at the table.

"Well, this is a guess, but the guy still sitting at the table is Ralph Mercer. He's an attorney. And from that wired guy's parting words and the fact that the only person to turn up dead within the last three days is Janice, I'd guess he wants some files from the attorney and Ralph isn't willing to give them up."

Our "doggy bags" came to the table, and they were the weirdest things I'd ever seen. Now, I hadn't eaten in very many fancy restaurants and this could have been standard, but have you ever had to take your leftover fettuccine home wrapped in foil shaped to look like a swan?

I got back to the conversation. My gaze moved from the swan to Ralph, who was still sitting over at his table as if too stunned to move. "That was kind of what I was thinking, too. But what kind of files? And the guy was pretty pissed when he stormed out. What could be so important that he would make such a huge deal of it in a restaurant?" It was something to think about. Right after I ate one more bite of the Death by Chocolate dessert on the china plate in front of me. Hence the to-go swan. I had my priorities, after all.

****

That night, after leaving Ben outside the front door, I savored the kiss he'd planted on me and kicked myself for still not feeling ready to jump him. What on earth was wrong with me? The man was practically everything I'd ever wanted, yet I wasn't going for it. I figured I'd chalk it up to temporary insanity.

I was so confused, and when you added the drama at the restaurant tonight, it didn't make for a peaceful night. I'd changed into a comfortable T-shirt and a pair of men's pajama pants. While brushing my teeth, I looked up into the mirror and something about the way the light hit my hair reminded me of Janice before she'd put on the wig to go with her costume.

Then it hit me. Could the angry man in the restaurant be the idiot customer she was talking about while I got her costume together? Could he be in town trying to get the files he hadn't paid for, the files Janice wouldn't give him when she was alive? Could he have killed her to get his hands on what he thought was his?

That kind of thinking could get me into trouble, though. I had no proof, and whoever heard of someone killing to get a company report back? I decided to put him and the murder out of my head for a little while. Until I had time to check out the identity of the angry man, I had nothing to go on. Who was I kidding? I had nothing to go on period, and no contacts within the police force to see if they had any leads, either.

I was still too wired to go to bed and found myself

firmly planted in front of the television, prone on the couch with a bowl of Cheetos in my hand. Nothing exciting was on, and my thoughts kept circling back to Ben. He had the greatest hands, and his smile could melt butter at thirty paces. Why would a hunk like that go after someone like me?

Certainly I wasn't a dog. I had dates in high school, although I hadn't had one in a while before leaving California. But that could have been because so many people in California were obsessed with weight. Malibu Barbie would fit right in.

I wasn't obsessed with losing weight myself—note the touching thighs and the need for sleeves at all times (no tank tops here)—and I certainly wasn't the thin model type. I'd always thought of myself more as the corn-fed variety of girl. So did that mean Ben liked his girls healthy, or was he feeling sorry for me, being the new girl and all? But then what about the attempt with the big words? I couldn't think straight.

When Harry Met Sally popped up on one of the cable stations, and I settled in to enjoy the whole friends-to-lovers thing, and especially the part with the faked orgasm in the deli. Maybe that could be Ben and me—the friends thing, not an orgasm at Mad Martha's Milk and Munchies.

On one side of my brain—the purely physical side—I wanted him with my every breath. But the other side, the one that said I'd waited this long, why not make sure it was really what I wanted before jumping in with both feet, was shouting louder and making more sense. I didn't want to make a mistake. This was a small town, and from what I'd already seen, few secrets were kept, much less hidden. Did I want my whole life to be laid out in front of everyone if things didn't go well with Ben?

But perhaps the whole small town thing wouldn't be so bad when trying to ferret out a murderer. Surely someone knew something that could help. I had to find out who, and how to pry the information from their brain.

I must have fallen asleep sometime after the part of the movie where Harry and Sally's newly married friends were arguing over the ugly wagon wheel coffee table, because when the phone rang, it jolted me off the couch and right onto the floor. Harry was running through the streets of New York trying to get to the New Year's Eve party and the ringing continued. I picked up the receiver right before it would have gone to voicemail, and after saying hello waited for whoever was on the line to do more than a heavy-breathing routine.

Chapter Sixteen

After a few seconds of what sounded like Lamaze (I was in the birthing room with my sister Maggie when she had her first munchkin), it occurred to me this could very well be an unfriendly phone call. Normally by now someone would have said they had the wrong number or at least hello. So I tried again. "Hello?"

Still nothing.

"Look if you're not going to say something, I'm hanging up. I don't go in for the whole phone-sex thing and have absolutely no interest in a new vacuum cleaner."

"Bitch," said a voice that was in no way nice. "Go home. We don't need some California slut running through this town."

"I am home." But the voice started the heavy breathing again, and I was a little scared. The threatening tone was so soft I couldn't tell if it was a man or a woman. The breathing continued, so I hung up with a definitive click. No one was going to make me think about leaving by calling me a bitch. And the slut part? Well, I thought my amazing resistance around Ben proved that false. Puh-lease, as Bella liked to say.

My backbone lasted through the thirty seconds it took for the phone to ring again. What if it was the voice again? What if the person on the phone said something meaner or more threatening? I thought long enough for the voicemail to pick up. Then I waited a couple of minutes for whoever it was to leave a message and hang up, before dialing my service number and retrieving the message. The whole "press one for unheard messages, press two for saved messages" thing played and my shaky finger pushed one.

There was a pause and then, "Hi Ivy, this is Maggie checking to see how you're settling in and wanting to warn you Dad is making plans to come out your way. He got this idea in his head that since you didn't come back in two weeks like he thought you would, he better come and get you."

No, no, no.

The message continued, "So brace yourself for the onslaught of Dad. Call me if you need anything. Love you, bye."

My dad was coming here? Here to my new house and my new shop with the boudoir in the back? Here to talk me out of my new life and back to his?

I was in some serious trouble. Stan Morris was nothing if not persuasive, and he could be very judgmental about things he didn't understand. He was not going to understand why I sold leather and vinyl bustiers for the dominatrix-inclined. This was not good.

The next morning, after a restless night with little to no sleep, I got out of bed and realized I'd better step up my morning routine if I wanted to get anything done before noon. Because the Halloween rush was over for my little costume shop and the Christmas season was not yet upon us (despite all the decorations going up in the big department stores an hour away), I was changing the store hours. Working seven days a week didn't allow me any kind of freedom, so I decided to close the shop on Tuesdays. An executive decision, for sure, but it wasn't like some of the people in town could like me less at this point. I had little to lose. Today was my first day of freedom.

Bella called to see what I was doing, right before I called her. For some reason, she said, her calendar was blocked off for today. She couldn't remember why she would have done that, but since she had nothing to do she wanted to get together. We agreed to meet up at her house and she'd come with me for my errands.

Well, now that I was going out with Bella, I had to wear something fancier than my blue jeans and a T-shirt. Bella never left the house if she was less than a hundred percent put together.

I chose a peacock blue silk T-shirt and black linen pants. I threw a long black sweater jacket over the whole thing and told myself I looked perfect.

The cold air was crisp as I walked the three short blocks to Bella's cottage. Fallen leaves crackled underfoot, and my heeled boots ate up the distance. There was something so exhilarating about the smell of wood smoke in the air and the bite of cold wind on my cheeks. The perverted and yucky caller of last night could shove it; my dad could take himself right back to where he came from. I was not leaving, and no one could make me.

When I arrived at Bella's house, it was a hive of activity. I knocked and there was no answer. I waited a minute, giving her a chance to come to the door, and then knocked again. Still no answer, so I let myself in.

My eyes must have been deceiving me, because I could have sworn I saw Bella running around with a makeup-free face and hair resembling a tumbleweed instead of her usual perfectly coiffed self. What had happened in the twenty minutes since I'd spoken to her?

I caught her on her second pass from the dining room to the kitchen, and she looked surprised to find someone gripping her arm. "Oh," she said, her mouth a perfect, naked O. "God, Ivy, you're already here. Didn't we just get off the phone?"

"Uh, no. That was almost thirty minutes ago." I peered around nervously at the mess in the living room and tried to shut out the loud music in the background. "What's going on?"

"I totally forgot about this makeover party I'm supposed to do tonight, and now I'm stuck. I'm trying to get things organized, and it's not coming together at all the way I thought it would. I'm in a panic."

"How about if I help you?" I asked, sincerely wanting to make her life a little easier. Bella had helped me out so many times and in so many ways the last few weeks. She'd been my first friend in this little town and my confidante when I'd needed her. And I knew, with my dad's imminent visit, I'd need her even more than before. So I threw on my best-friend hat and waited for her to tell me to go do any number of things.

But all she came up with was, "Can you make some coffee?"

"Sure. But isn't there anything else I can do to help at the same time? I'm actually a pretty good organizer after years of practice in the corporate world. Can't I do anything more substantial for you?"

"Believe me, coffee is not only substantial but crucial at this point in time. If you can get some started,

I'd be forever grateful, and then we'll see what else you can do to help." The absent smile was so unlike Bella I didn't know what else to do but go and start the coffee.

After putting the paper cone in the Mr. Coffee and pouring in grounds I finally found in the freezer, I pushed the glowing red button and went to find Bella.

"So why all the craziness?" I asked, after locating her out on the little back patio that looked out over a lush and colorful garden of roses and aged trees.

"I guess with Janice's death this party totally slipped my mind. If nothing else, I would have thought it would be cancelled, since it's Janice's aunt that's throwing it."

"I hadn't realized Janice had any family here. I thought she'd moved here last year to get away from family."

Bella sat heavily in a chaise lounge and I followed suit in the matching chair. "Well, now, I wouldn't really call it family in the way that you or I might think of family. It's a very strange combination of hate and jealousy and family obligation. Janice moved back last year because her uncle had been diagnosed with colon cancer. She felt she should be here for the uncle and to help her aunt, since Janice's cousins couldn't seem to tear themselves away from the jet-setting scene in South Florida. So Janice showed up in town and stayed with her aunt for about a week before it was apparent that living there would be like asking for a front row seat in hell."

"Huh. I guess that would be a hard situation to move into."

"That's not the half of it. Janice had to sit all the time and listen to how perfect the cousins were, even when she'd been the one to move half way across the country and they still hadn't come home. Here their mother is, trying to help her husband, and it's their father who is dying, but they can't be bothered because it's the height of the season down there." Flipping some of her mussed hair out of her eyes, she got up from her chair and stalked to the kitchen for the fresh coffee. I followed again.

Bella poured herself a huge ceramic mug full, took a sip, and turned back toward me. "Ooohhh. That is so much better." She took another sip before continuing. "So anyway, about ten months ago the uncle passed, the kids finally got their act together enough to at least come for the funeral, and the will was read. The shit absolutely hit the fan. The uncle had left Janice a very tidy sum of money and the kids were fighting tooth and nail to get it back. Said it was theirs and she had no right to anything. But the aunt was the loudest because the money actually came out of her stuff. The kids won't really get anything until both parents pass away. So not only were the cousins pissed Janice got something, they were also pissed because they still have to wait for their mother to go to the great shopping mall beyond before they see any of their money."

"Sheesh. That's pretty selfish. Especially when they hadn't done anything at all. And besides, it was the uncle's money."

"Right you are, Miss Ivy, but not in the cousins' eyes." Bella walked over to the sofa and started counting brushes and packets of test eye shadow. "As far as they were concerned, Janice was a freeloader and a gold digger, if you can believe it."

I gasped and couldn't help myself—I laughed. Not

in a "ha-ha this is funny" kind of way, but in the way that bursts from you when you simply cannot believe someone did something so totally outrageous. "God, that is some serious nerve."

"You're not kidding me. Janice was really upset and decided to not have anything to do with them for the last few months. But then her aunt called her, wanting to reconcile, and Janice was a really big softy at heart. So she went over to the family house and tried to bridge the gap between them. Janice is...was such a sucker for a contrite heart. Even if it turned out her aunt really wasn't sorry."

More packets of eye shadow and blush were sifted through and the piles grew, teetering and then settling into a kind of small mountain. Even with my unpracticed eye I could see Bella was sorting by tones, and I was impressed. I think that's another reason I had liked always wearing brown; it's hard to screw up in coordinating outfits when everything goes with everything else.

I missed Janice and had only known her for a short while. I couldn't even imagine what it was like for Bella. "I'm really sorry, Bella. I hadn't realized you and Janice were such good friends."

"Not so much good friends. She came into the shop every six weeks for a trim, and we got to know each other. But I will really miss her as a customer. She was fun and great to talk to." A sigh escaped Bella and it was weary, heavy. "But back to her aunt. Well, that is one chilly woman. She called this morning to make sure we were still on schedule for the party, like nothing new had come up since she planned this ridiculous little soiree. Can you believe it's supposed to be for some other biddy's birthday? I could understand a day at the spa, or everyone going to a salon for the works. But a makeover party in your home? Maybe with a Mary Kay consultant, but I was trying to do a favor for Janice, and now I have to go regardless of how much I want to punch that rude bitch aunt in the face."

"Would you like some help? Not with the punching in the face thing but with the party?"

"Well, there's not a whole lot to do, but it would be nice to have the support. You could hold back my fist if she says something snarky."

"It would be my pleasure. So what time is this soiree?"

****

Two hours later, I'd run my errand at the dry cleaners and stopped by the police station to find out if there was anything else they needed from me regarding the costume I'd turned in. The answer there was No and a polite, "Keep your nose out of this." Fine, then, I thought at the time. But I really wanted to find out what was going on, so I made a mental note to tap Ben's brain and connections.

Bella and I jumped into her bright yellow VW Bug after we'd packed the trunk with every kind of cosmetic available, and we headed out for the aunt's house.

"All right," Bella said with a sneer on her perfectly made-up face and a toss of her perfectly coiffed hair. (I felt much better now that she was back to the Bella I knew and loved. Not that I begrudge a person a day minus the makeup, but it was a little disconcerting to see her so frazzled when she always seemed so put together.)

"This party is a birthday party—remind me never

to allow myself to be roped into one of these things again. We'll set up two different stations and have a line of women going from the makeup to the hair. They have to do their own makeup and the hair will be my thing. Your only job is to make sure they don't swipe a whole bunch of the packets I put in the baskets. I once had one of these things with eight people. I brought forty packets, expecting a big turnout, and even though I should have walked home with a bunch of stuff left over, those women completely cleaned me out. So keep a sharp eye on them."

"Will do."

We pulled up at a brick ranch-style house with every window aglow. The sound of cackling women drifting from the house as we got out of the car reminded me of the Shakespeare tale about the three witches. I really hoped I wouldn't "toil and trouble" while here tonight.

I helped Bella with the cargo in the back. We each took an armful of capes, tablecloths, and the baskets of cellophane-wrapped and bundled clusters of every combination of eye shadow, blush, lipstick, mascara, and foundation packets.

A short, blue-haired lady answered our knock. If this was the aunt, she was seriously a cool cucumber. No nice smile or handshaking, no "Thanks for coming." Instead we got "What the hell took you so long? You better not be late setting up."

We followed as she went into a dark room and threw on the lights, revealing a whole lot of chintz and shelf upon shelf of knick-knacks. I was feeling claustrophobic already. Bella set up a table in the corner as the merry aunt went about, sniffing periodically and harrumphing often.

"Would you mind getting me a glass of soda, Mildred?" Bella asked, causing the look on the woman's face to go from mere disapproval all the way to fierce scowl. But she did move, after a stare down between her and Bella, in which Mildred looked away first. She clomped away on her orthopedic shoes, and there was about thirty seconds of silence before I had to muffle a giggle.

"Holy cow," I said, still trying to keep the laughter inside. It certainly wouldn't do for Mildred to walk back in while I was laughing like a loon.

"Yeah," Bella said, fighting a battle of her own and obviously losing. "Why me?"

"Oh, I don't know. She seemed sweet on you."

"Yeah, right. You think maybe it's the stick up her ass that makes her look so anal?"

"Bella!"

"What?"

"She could walk in any minute. You don't want her to discreetly hock a loogie into your soda pop before she gives it to you, do you?"

"She wouldn't even dream of that."

"But you can't be sure. I'd like to get in and out of here with the least amount of trouble possible. I have to open tomorrow and do not want to have a bunch of old women at my door telling me I'm a terrible person and they'll never come in my shop again. Some of the older women are the ones I usually find in the back of the shop holding up panties with less fabric than is truly advisable for someone of that advanced age."

Just then Aunt Mildred walked back in with two glasses filled with dark liquid and put them on the third table in the room. "If you're finished setting up," she paused significantly, like master to servant, "we're ready to begin this part of the evening."

For the next hour and a half, I eyed the basket of samples and how many each person was taking while Bella worked on up-dos, beehives, and perfect pin curls.

I'd heard some gossip this evening but nothing that really gave me any clues as to who had killed Janice. I wasn't any closer on where to start my search.

One last lady came by my table, picked up a neutral/brown packet, and headed over to Bella. The gaunt woman sat in the makeshift salon chair in front of Bella and started talking. I was arranging the leftover sample packets (yes, with my eagle eye there were leftovers) to go back to the car, when the older woman started talking. "Such a shame about Janice. It's too bad Ralph Mercer couldn't get that awful client of hers to go home. I heard the client threatened Ralph with a lawsuit, as if he could be intimidated. This guy has been causing a heap of trouble around here. Poor Martha Howard over at Mad Martha's has had to put up with his snotty attitude every morning since Thursday, and Nancy Harkham at the Bubbling Brook is housing him. He is not a nice man."

After Bella explained to the newbie (namely me) that the full name for the establishment was the Bubbling Brook Bed and Breakfast, I paused, a little awestruck. Two things concerned me from this conversation. One: the guy was in the area during the murder and had now moved up to my number one suspect. Two: was this town unable to name anything without using a heavy hand with the alliteration?

Chapter Seventeen

As Bella teased and rat-tailed the woman's hair, they talked and talked. But my mind was stuck on the whole client-being-in-town thing. The same client who had threatened Janice days ago had shown up not twenty-four hours before she was killed. Coincidence? I didn't think so.

I tuned back into the conversation in time to hear the woman praise Bella for her expertise with the comb and promise to make another appointment for the following week. Shortly after, she left the room and Bella and I were alone.

"I really love these old ladies. Where would I be without their weekly appointments for a wash and set?" A beatific smile flashed across Bella's face before it turned into a smirk, and then out-and-out laughter.

"You are terrible."

"I'm not terrible, Ivy, I'm honest. These parties are hard for me to stomach but they always get me at least one new client, and it seems I'm handy with a comb."

We cleaned up the room, putting furniture back onto the grooves in the carpet and straightening the doilies on the end tables. We made a last check for anything we'd missed and walked down the short hallway to the front door. I waited there while Bella went and said goodbye to Mildred. My eyes were about to roll back in my head from staring at the entire Annie plate collection from the 1970s when finally Bella came out with a smile on her face and a swing in her hips.

"We're flush," she said and stuffed a handful of bills in the neck of my shirt.

"What?"

"I said, we're flush. Mildred and her friends all thought we were worth their time and money and tipped generously. Let's go to the bar."

Ten minutes later, we were comfortably seated in the captain's chairs, which I was becoming quite fond of, with drinks in hand. Now if Ben would only show up tonight and maybe sweep me off my feet again with his version of dancing. That is, if I could keep from falling head first into his lap.

"You're thinking about Ben again, aren't you?"

"How do you do that?" It was becoming a habit for Bella to read my expression, or was she really psychic? Psychic would definitely help me find my missing lingerie and get a bead on who did it.

"Do what?" she asked.

"Know what I'm thinking."

"Oh, that. Well, part of it is from doing hair and seeing so many women and their different moods. The other part is I know you and you get this dreamy, disgusting look on your face whenever you are thinking about him or chocolate. And since you have a slice of Death by Chocolate in front of you and some smeared around your mouth, I figured it had to be Ben."

I quickly took a swipe at my mouth with a napkin. How embarrassing. "Are you sure you're not psychic?"

"I wish. If I could predict the numbers or see into the future or past or whatever it is they do, I'd be at the convenience store so fast your pretty head of highlights would spin."

"Would you give up the salon if you won the lottery?" I took a sip of my drink, Premium Plum, and waited for her answer. She took a very long time to decide.

"I don't think I'd want to give up the shop. It's what I've done for so long I'd be lost without it. But would I hire some more people to do the actual cutting and stuff? Take a vacation at least once a month to some exotic place with tall fruity drinks and even taller, sexy cabana boys? You bet your ass I would." She tossed off the rest of her watermelon shooter and chased it with beer, which I still hadn't figured out how to do gracefully. The first time I'd tried, the night I met Ben (and I made a conscious effort not to get the fool smile on my face this time), I'd tried a shooter and ended up with more on my napkin bib than in my mouth. Yes, napkin bib. Bella knew me well enough even then.

Music started on the jukebox, some old Western song. I had no idea what the person was singing, but I believe most of it was about dead or faithful dogs and lying or wayward women who done him wrong. Bella got up from her chair and started weaving around to the music. It looked like she was going to try to pull me with her, until a strong hand settled on my shoulder.

"I could smell your fragrance from the door. Something about you draws me right to wherever you are."

I turned around to tell Ben what a line of bullshit *that* was and he kissed me. End of conversation.

I walked home from Bella's, thinking about the kiss from Ben and the way it had made my head swirl.

He should be declared illegal and left at that. There was something about him and his smooth ways that made me want to swoon at his feet. But there was something about me, too. Maybe it was my newly forming backbone that made me feel I should resist him and all the sexual delights he could bring to the table, or, er, the bed. I didn't know if I was ready for a table thing before I tried out the bed. I mean, would I be sexy laid out on the table like a Butterball turkey?

Perhaps not. So we could start out in the bedroom, preferably with the lights off and the curtains shut against the moonlight. God, was I so conventional it even had to take place at night? Maybe my backbone wasn't meant to include forays into the more adventurous side of sexual escapades.

Sometimes I wished I could be more like Bella and go after what I wanted. But then I thought about the responsibility and the effort involved in doing what I wanted all the time, and shied away. I did not want to be "on" all the time.

A shout and a thud turned my attention from my thoughts. A guy stood on a doorstep across the street and a police officer staggered back, almost falling off the stoop. The cop saved himself from the fall at the last possible second, and I breathed a sigh of relief.

Suddenly it struck me that the guy still standing on the doorstep, his shoulders rising and falling in great heaving waves, was the same man as in last night's dining experience at the restaurant. What the hell was going on?

Against my better judgment I walked over to the other side of the street. I tried to look like your average walker and not give a hint I was eavesdropping as the cop yanked the other man's hands behind his back and started leading him to the squad car sitting at the curb.

"You're an idiot! They're mine, and I will have them," the cuffed man screamed.

"Well, you're lucky you didn't land a better punch, because I'm already pissed off enough to throw you in jail and leave you there to rot for assaulting an officer. Get in the car without a fuss and I might remember to let you eat sometime tomorrow."

"I demand you take me back to my cabin this instant. Who the hell do you think you are?"

"Look, buddy, I'm the guy who's hauling your ass to jail. You won't be going back to your cabin, wherever it is, because you're spending the night in jail, and maybe the remainder of the week if you don't keep your trap shut."

I looked at the house again after the cop drove away with the guy in the back seat. I realized I was on the same street Bella said Janice had lived on. The front, with its raspberry gingerbread trim and moss green woodwork, looked exactly like the description Bella had given me when I asked her about it. And if this was Janice's house, and a man who looked familiar to me had been standing on the stoop with a cop arguing about something of his, I'd bet dollars to doughnuts the guy was the infamous threatening client.

Despite the fact I already had a suspect, kind of, in Mr. Jorgensen of the bloodstained cape, I still didn't want it to be him. I'd be much more comfortable putting this murder on someone else. Someone I was already inclined not to like.

Things were adding up in my head for the client to be the guilty party. He'd threatened Janice, threatened the lawyer, and now assaulted a policeman, all in the name of some files that were supposedly his. Ones no one would give to him. What in the files was so all-important? And if he wanted them so badly, would he kill for them?

I ran the rest of the way home, hoping to clear my head of the two drinks I'd had at the bar, and slammed the front door behind me after whipping up the porch steps like someone was hot on my tail. I had a plan brewing in my head, but I'd need to change clothes before I started the execution.

****

I felt like it was amateur night at a Goth club. I'd pulled my hair back and up into a black watch cap and donned black sweats and a dark blue windbreaker. I stopped short of putting black stripes under my eyes and instead ended up lining them with a kohl pencil. I am Barbarella, hear me roar.

Not. More like Spazzarella.

The Bubbling Brook Bed and Breakfast was far enough away from my house to use the car. Besides, I didn't want to get caught wandering around town dressed all in black. Someone might think I was going on a burglarizing spree, or turning to the dark side.

They wouldn't be half wrong. I was planning on some burglary, just not a spree. Simply one room at ye old B&B. I hadn't worked out how I was going to get in yet, but I figured now, when the client was down at the police station, would be the perfect time to see if there was anything worthy of attention in his room.

I didn't want to park right up in the half-moon drive in front of the B&B. No one was supposed to know I had even been here, so I certainly didn't want to park my car out front for everyone to see. I found a little bald spot on the side of the road, surrounded by tall trees, directly after the three-story Victorian house that was the Bubbling Brook B & B. Pulling the car into the makeshift parking spot, I checked my flashlight and grabbed the only tool I'd found at home, a screwdriver. I crept away from the car and up to the imposing building. How was I even going to know what room the client was in? And how would I get up there without being heard? Okay, maybe I hadn't planned this very well.

Most of the downstairs lights were off, leaving the front lawn bathed only in moonlight. No clouds hung in the cold, clear sky. The scent of more wood smoke teased my nose, and an image of me in front of a roaring fire with a cup of hot chocolate and a good book almost sent me running back to my car and my house.

But my determination to find out who'd cut down Janice in her prime was stronger than my need for comfort right now. So I crept forward and prayed the stairs leading to the porch wouldn't squeak.

Of course they protested loudly. I tried hopping lightly from one foot to the other to maybe find a spot without a chorus to follow when a light popped on in what I assumed was a foyer of some kind.

As I was about to turn tail and run, the porch light flickered. Caught. Shit. So much for my burglary skills. I'd have to stick with my day job.

"Ivy? Ivy Morris is that you?" A quiet voice came out of the light and startled me into moving.

"Ah, yes." Hurry, hurry, need to find an excuse fast. "I was out for a, um, walk and was wondering if I could use your bathroom." That had to be the most asinine thing I'd ever said. Surprisingly, it seemed to work, because the gray-haired lady, who I quickly remembered as Mrs. Nancy Harkham, led me to a small powder room under the stairs rising to the second floor.

I really did have to go to the bathroom after that nerve-wracking encounter. Stalling for time, I finished washing my hands and tried to think up a way to find out which room the guy was staying in.

While looking in the mirror at myself to check how wacky my makeup really looked, my brain made a connection I hadn't thought of. When he was being hauled away, the guy made a comment about staying at a cabin and Ben had mentioned the B&B had a small freestanding building they called "The Cabin." They used it as a honeymoon suite.

My life got a little easier. I didn't have to figure out how to sneak back into the B & B because the cottage was across the driveway and tucked into a group of trees. Things were finally going my way.

With a fast wave and a heartfelt "thank you" to Mrs. Harkham, I hustled out the door like I was continuing some kind of after-midnight power walk and stopped at my car.

I let ten minutes pass before I tried to get on the property again. Long enough for all the lights to turn off.

Long enough for me to wonder what kind of town this was when a bathroom stop at your local hotel in the middle of the night didn't even cause a person to blink. Seriously to my advantage, but bizarre.

The moon was still shining brightly in the sky, but a cloud hovered to its left. I waited another minute and was rewarded when the cloud moved across the bright globe and dimmed the light. I walked slowly, so as not to make a lot of rustling, and approached the gravel drive. Staying on the grass, I carefully made my way to the cabin and found all the lights off. This was good. No way had the police taken the client guy into custody and already released him. I was safe for the moment.

My plan was to get in and get out as quickly as possible. I had no idea what I was actually looking for but figured I would know it when I saw it.

The front door faced away from the bed and breakfast. Privacy was also good. Now no one would be able to see me trying to open the door, which could be a little difficult considering I hadn't thought about the fact that it was probably locked.

Banging my head on the wall in frustration was out of the question, so I settled on a few moments of vivid cursing under my breath.

How could I be so stupid? Did I think I was going to waltz up to the door and it would magically be unlocked, ready for me to walk right in and look around? Dammit.

I was about to turn around and go back to the car to look for something to help me pop the lock, since the screwdriver jammed in my back pocket would be useless, when I heard a sound off to my left. Thick trees stood in a large line like a barrier to the forest beyond, and the sound had originated from that direction. Maybe.

I stuck to the shadows on the porch of the cabin and waited for whomever or, gulp, whatever had made the sound to either go away or show itself. I voted for go away, and kept a sharp ear out for any other noise indicating the person or thing was moving back into the shelter of the forest.

No sound came, and I felt a sigh of relief swelling in my chest right before a hand clamped over my mouth.

Chapter Eighteen

The hand clamped down a little harder as I refilled my lungs to scream. Even if it came out muffled, I decided I'd try to let loose a noise that would wake the whole neighborhood and possibly the dead. Then I heard a familiar voice speak in my ear.

"Don't scream, Ivy. Let's save that for the bedroom."

I whirled around and punched Ben in the stomach. A muffled "umph" came from those delicious lips as he doubled over. "You idiot," I hissed. "You nearly scared the pee out of me. What the hell is your problem?"

But Ben still seemed beyond speech as he looked at me with hurting eyes. I'd give him hurting eyes. He'd better just be happy I didn't aim lower and with my knee.

He straightened a little and looked like an aerobics instructor trying to work out the kinks. "What was that for?" he said, trying to pull the whole wounded-person thing.

"I told you what it was for. Never, never, creep up on me and scare me like that again. You're lucky I didn't aim for your balls." His eyes widened, and I clamped my hand over my mouth. I had not, in any way, shape, or form, meant to say that out loud.

Maybe the backbone was growing a little faster than I had originally thought. I'd never said balls to an actual man before. Sure, I'd said it in the office restroom after some idiot talked down to me or one of the male assistants decided to make some kind of snide remark about my weight or lack of a boyfriend. But never to someone's face before. Was I supposed to apologize now? No, I didn't think I wanted to. What I needed to do was change the subject.

"What are you doing here?" I whispered.

"I was going to ask you the same question."

"Well, I asked you first. And don't try arguing with me right now. What are you doing here?"

In the same hushed voice that sent shivers up my spine, he said, "Oh, all right. I came over because I heard the police had picked up the client guy on assault charges and I knew he wouldn't be here for a while. I thought I'd do a little bit of investigating on my own. Now you?"

"What, did you finally finish your online class and decide to break in your new private investigator license?"

The one cloud in the sky shifted and the full round moon shone down on Ben's face. It looked like he was actually blushing. Blushing? That was too rich. "You did, didn't you? You got your license and wanted to try it out, so you what? Listened to the police scanner that everyone seems to have in this town and came down here to see what the guy was up to yourself?"

"I don't hear you answering my question."

I snickered. "You're not going to hear me answer your question until you tell me whether or not this foray into investigating was brought on by you receiving your new license."

"Okay, okay. Yes, I got my new license this

afternoon. It's actually a temporary one for right now. And yes, I did hear the cops saying they'd picked up Mr. Samuel Hedlund, also known as 'that client guy,' trying to get into Janice's house. I heard he threw a punch at Dennis, which is never a good idea. I went to high school with Dennis, and he has a jaw of iron. There was this kid he fought once, and the kid actually broke his hand when it connected with Dennis's jawbone, and Dennis didn't even stagger. Of course, I could always take him down when we were in wrestling together. It didn't take much to get him in a headlock."

"Oh, now there's a picture I simply will not be able to get out of my head. You and another guy in those tight leotard-type outfits with your arms around each other. Nice. Did you have the head gear, too?"

"Of course we had the head...ha, ha, ha. You're a funny one. Fine, go ahead and make fun of me all you want, but I looked good in that outfit. It showed off my ass to perfection."

I rolled my eyes and finally remembered where we were—in the middle of breaking and entering into a guest's cabin at the local bed and breakfast. Yet here we were playing getting-to-know-you games. I stuck my elbow out to get his attention and he neatly sidestepped me this time.

"I don't fall for that twice. Should I be grateful you didn't go for my balls this time, too?"

I blushed and hoped the cloud cover had moved back across the moon to hide the flaming hot skin from my neck to my forehead.

"Ivy, seriously, you should go home. I can take care of this. There's no need for both of us to get into trouble for checking this guy out."

I stared at him in disbelief. I had gotten here first, I was trying to figure out a way in, and now Mr. Wrestler was telling me (me!) to go home like a good little girl and let the big bad man take care of things. How dare he!

"How dare you!" My anger got the best of me and my voice got a little louder than I would have hoped.

"Let's use our inside voices, Ivy."

I hit him in the arm this time for his condescending comment. And since when was I so physically violent? What happened to that strong filter I'd boasted about between my head and abuse? Regardless, it got his attention.

"Ow, again. Do you make it a habit to hit people who are trying to look out for your best interests?"

"No, I do not make it a habit to hit people who are looking out for my best interests, but I do hit people who are patronizing me. Why should I go away? Why don't you go away?"

"You have got to be kidding me. I'm not going away. And if you're not going away, then at least get behind me while I jimmy this lock."

"Then we'll be partners, right? I'll help you, you'll help me, and we share all information."

"Uh, yeah, sure," Ben said as he opened this black velvet case-like pouch with a bunch of shiny tools inside. He drew out a long slim tool and examined it.

I was about to let him do his thing when his answer sank into my head. I put out a hand to block the lock and keep him from trying his luck with it until I got some clear, definite promise from him that we were in this together.

"You want to move out of the way so I can get us

in before sunrise?"

"No, I do not want to move. I want you to tell me we are going to be partners in this. I'm not going home to twiddle my thumbs like some dumb girl while you go do your manly-man thing and leave me in the dark."

"I wasn't planning on leaving you in the dark, as you say. I think it's too dangerous for you to be sticking your nose in things you don't know anything about."

"And you know all about investigating because you got some piece of paper from the Internet." That was so rude I started apologizing immediately, even before I saw the look of hurt flit across his face. "I'm sorry, Ben. That was wrong of me. I don't know what's gotten into me today. First I say 'balls' to a man and then I insult you." Oops, hadn't meant to say that part about the balls. But without trying, I seemed to have diffused some of the tension.

"You've never said balls to a guy before?"

I did not want to continue this conversation, but I felt maybe I owed it to him after the bitchy Internet paper comment. "No, I haven't." That was all I would say about it. The end.

"Never? That's a pretty long time. You didn't say it to some guy in the eighth grade because he was trying to pinch you or something?"

Apparently not the end. "No, I guess it never came up. Besides, I'm still waiting for you to agree to be partners before I move. Let's keep focused on the important issues and stop talking about your balls." God, did it get any worse than this?

He looked me over for a minute and finally nodded. "We'll let go of the balls conversation and concentrate on the important things. Why do you think I should let a total amateur help me with this when I can do it myself?"

I held my tongue as another snide comment about his dubious (oh, good word, Ivy) use of his qualifications came to mind. "I think you should let me help you because I can be an extra set of eyes, ears, and hands. A lot of customers who come in spend time gossiping. I can pick up any interesting information and pass it on to you. I doubt you have many drop-ins at the newspaper."

"Like an extra set of hands, huh?"

Trust a man to zero in on that part. "I also found some evidence with a direct bearing on the murder." Never mind that I wasn't entirely sure if the blood on the cape had anything to do with Janice, because the police hadn't seen fit to give me any kind of update. But I didn't let that little bump in the road stop me.

"What kind of evidence?" He stopped and shook his head. "You know what, it doesn't matter. If I can't get through to the lock soon, I'll lose my chance to see what this guy is hiding. I guess I'll have to agree to whatever you say."

"I need to hear the words." My hands had moved to my hips.

"Fine. I agree to be partners with you. Now please move your cute ass out of my way so I can get at this lock."

I had a cute ass? I resisted the urge to twist around and check it out for myself as Ben got to work on the door.

He grabbed the knob and moved to put the first tool between the door and the jamb. The door simply creaked open. "Well, shit."

I laughed and got a narrow-eyed look for my insubordination. "So, master detective, I guess we should have tried the door before breaking out the tools."

"The tools are fine. I should have tried the door before agreeing to your stupid partner thing."

Ben was still rubbing his arm where I'd swatted him for a second time when we made our way into the cabin. The floor plan was simple: one big room housed a bed and sitting area, a small kitchenette, and a café style table for two. Nothing looked out of place and the king-sized bed was perfectly made.

I was just happy no one had been here before us. And hopefully no one would come in while we were doing our search.

"You take the bathroom," Ben said in a whisper. That whisper was doing some serious things to my libido, even when he was cursing at me. Yes, I figured I was perverse.

I didn't want to argue now that we were actually inside and able to see if there were any clues here. So I took myself to the bathroom and started my search while I heard faint noises coming from the main part of the cabin.

The small bath smelled like Old English but was actually quite neat for a guy. A comb and a bottle of gel were lined up on the white counter. No stubble was lying around the rim of the sink, and the tube of toothpaste actually had the cap on. Plus, no ring of urine around the toilet.

If I hadn't thought this guy was a murderer, I'd be tempted to see if he was available. I mean, cleanliness was next to sexiness for dating material, as far as I was concerned. I sure hoped Ben wasn't a slob.

Ten minutes later, we both came back to the center of the main room, shaking our heads. "I didn't find anything," I said. "I looked through the bathroom cabinets and found the normal stuff. It looks like he's settled in here for a little while. He has everything unpacked and his travel bag is stuffed under the sink. He's neat and not a thing is out of place." Actually, looking at how neat he was had me rethinking the whole cleanliness thing. Even *I* wasn't that organized, and I didn't think I could be with someone who made sure all the labels on his toiletries faced the same way and were alphabetized. It was a little scary and a lot anal-retentive, now that I'd thought about it.

"I didn't find anything either," Ben said. His shirt was coming untucked and his brown hair was mussed, like he'd run his fingers through it several times in the short while we'd been here. His fingers forked through the strands again, confirming my suspicion. "This guy is way too organized and didn't bring anything with him besides two pairs of pants, two shirts, socks, funky orange-striped underwear, and his bathroom stuff. No books, no files, no incriminating evidence. Crap." Ben shook his head and jammed his hands in his pockets. "Dammit," he said. "I was so sure he'd have some kind of secret stash of things hidden in his clothes or in a drawer that would link him to Janice's death."

"I know. I've looked in every nook and cranny."

His head snapped up. "But I haven't." He stalked over to the small kitchenette and opened the cupboards under the sink. Wedging himself into the tiny space, only his stomach, waist and legs were visible as he wiggled around looking for something, anything.

Chapter Nineteen

A couple of minutes later I heard Ben's muffled voice from under the sink. "Yes." His tall, lean body wiggled out from beneath the counter and I was treated to a view that made my mouth water. Each delicious inch came out from under the sink—broad chest, well-defined arms, nice shoulder. The chin I wanted to nibble, the mouth I wanted to bite, the eyes I think I fell into when we first met, despite my horribly embarrassing run to the bathroom. Why wasn't I sleeping with him? At that moment I had no idea what was holding me back, and if we had been in a different place, say a bed, and not breaking and entering in a possible murderer's room, I'd have jumped Ben Fallon the Fallen.

"What? What? What's a yes?" I said, dragging my mind back to the matter at hand.

I think some of my intense perusal and subsequent arousal must have come across to him, because as soon as he scooted out completely his green eyes zeroed in on me. Then that smile, that killer smile, widened into a devilish grin. "Exciting, isn't it?"

And what was I supposed to say to that? "Sure it is. We're in someone else's room, uninvited, and you found something you don't seem to be sharing. What's more exciting than that?"

"You're not that oblivious, but I'll let it go this

time." He paused to look me over and I hoped like hell my nipples weren't peaked under my black top. At least not to the extent that he could see them. "I found this folder taped up under the sink. Do you want to look at it here or go to my house and finish what we've started?"

Well, that was certainly a double entendre if I ever heard one, and I spent about a half second deciding what I wanted from Ben and for myself. I was tired of playing this never-ending game in my head. I knew the important parts of him, and maybe if we got the deed done I wouldn't feel so out of sorts, so off balance. And wasn't that a lovely way to think of ending my long run on celibacy?

But I said the words and then there was no turning back. "Let's go to your house."

Following Ben in my car, I felt my stomach start to knot with dread and anticipation. Was I ready for this? What was I getting myself into? Had I shaved my legs?

A quick feel under the leg of my pants answered the last question in the affirmative and left me with only the two other questions. I'd been drawn to Ben since the first time we met, which I admitted wasn't so long ago. But something about him really pulled at me. He was funny, charming, and sexy. He made me feel sexy. That was a serious point in his favor.

Five minutes later we pulled up in front of one of three apartment buildings in town. I parked in a spot close to the entrance, right next to Ben. We both got out of our cars at the same time, and Ben came around his hood to take my hand. Who knew holding hands could be so seductive? I felt a tingle from my toes straight to the roots of my hair and worried I might pass out if he actually touched one of my erogenous zones. Would I faint dead away? Perhaps, but it sure would be fun to experience.

We walked into a foyer and up the stairs directly in front of us, Ben tugging me along behind him. "This is home sweet home," he said in that sardonic voice which always made me want to listen to more of his dry wit.

"It's a nice building," I said, for lack of anything better. My mind flashed back to my little cottage and how much I loved it. Truthfully, though, I would have lived anywhere in order to live outside my father's house and that damn pink room. Maybe I wasn't the right person to remark on anyone's living situation.

"Yes, it is a nice building, but I'd give it up in a heartbeat if I could live in a house like yours. Plenty of room to stretch out, no one to bang on the walls if you're making too much noise. A yard."

"You say yard like it's the Holy Grail."

"Well, I have a secret," he said in a whisper, making my body automatically lean in closer to hear this secret. "I really shouldn't tell you. You may use it against me."

"I will not." I found I was also whispering and it took some of the starch out of the indignant, fierce way I'd wanted to speak.

His eyebrow quirked at me and, as if he hadn't already had enough intriguing attributes, this was one more thing that made my mouth go dry. I'd always admired anyone who had such control over their facial features, but on Ben it was especially sexy.

"I won't," I said, louder this time.

"Well, my secret is..." He leaned in closer and I could feel his breath on my neck, like a hot caress. His nose tickled the outer shell of my ear and I almost fainted dead away, I was so turned on. And now it was confirmed, I was probably going to die when his hands actually managed to touch any area that was supposed to turn my knees to water. I was so screwed—hopefully, literally. "I like to get my hands dirty...planting flowers."

"Mmmm." It was a sexual, throaty noise until what he'd actually said took root in my brain. Uh, flowers? Okay that was so not what I thought I'd hear. "Huh?"

"Flowers. I know it's not very manly, but I really like the feel of the earth in my hands and putting geraniums in a pot isn't quite the same. Have you seen Bella's gardens? What I wouldn't give for a space like that to really dig into." On his face was a smile I had only ever associated with orgasm, and we were talking about flowers and dirt. "Huh" was right.

"Of course my other passion involves getting dirty with something a little more sweaty and geared toward the bedroom or a convenient floor."

Now there was the Ben I knew and loved. Loved? No, liked a lot, though. Enough that I thought I wanted to see if we could figure out how best to go at it on the floor without one or both of us ending up with some nasty rug burn. And despite those naughty thoughts I was pretty sure I still blushed.

"So on to the envelope we confiscated from Mr. Hedlund. Let's open it up and see what was so secret he had to hide it under a sink, in an envelope, and practically glued shut."

Ben worked on the closed envelope while I wandered around a bit. His apartment wasn't exactly bachelor-pad material, as he had some really nice antique pieces. A beautiful armoire stood at the wall in the living room and, of course, housed a larger than average television along with a big collection of DVDs and CDs. Then there were the video game systems; the man had everything since the Atari came out, and games to go with each of them. Typical male.

A piecrust table held a disreputable and scarred wooden bowl filled with keys and change. A Tiffany-style lamp sat on a nicely aged leather-topped table, which brought me to the couch. Were guys incapable of having a place to sit that did not involve the use of duct tape? The monstrosity in the middle of the living room was some horrid orange-and-green plaid pattern from the seventies and needed, desperately, to hit the garbage dump. Not even a cover could save the soul of that poor thing. But over in the corner Ben had a brand-new-looking recliner in a plush sand color. Brown. My kind of guy.

Ben made a humming noise while he tried to pry the rest of the tape off the flap of the envelope without tearing the paper.

"Any luck?" I said as I turned from a collection of pictures on the mantel. All had Ben with a woman or women in some wilderness-looking setting, and I didn't want to contemplate how many of those women were not related to him.

"Almost got it," he said as he worked a knife under the edge of the flap. "Finally. Now come on over here, Ivy. Let's see what the client guy was hiding." When I hesitated with my hand on the back of the ugly couch, he laughed. "I won't bite unless you ask."

"Ha, ha, now shut up and let's see what we found."

"We found? I specifically remember I was the one to crawl under that awful sink, and please remind me to tell Nancy she should have her worker bees clean under there a little better next time. I almost made contact with a used condom and was not happy."

"Oh, poor baby. How will you explain why you were under there? Now hurry, I'm getting impatient waiting to see what *we* found."

Carefully, Ben shook out the contents of the envelope and we stared, horrified at what fell onto the table.

Chapter Twenty

"Okay, no one that skinny should ever have naked pictures taken of themselves," I said as I struggled not to laugh my ass off.

"Uh, yeah, I completely agree, these are totally wrong in every sense of the word."

It seemed the vocal Mr. Client Guy might have had another reason for being in town, a reason he was covering up for by making a big fuss about Janice and his files. Or maybe there was something on one of the files Janice had that would be incriminating. Either way, I was pretty sure we'd tracked the wrong rabbit.

"Do you think he was being blackmailed?" Ben asked, stuffing back into the manila envelope the nudie pictures of a very skinny client guy and an extremely tiny, curvy blonde getting it on.

"I can't think of what else the note we found in the envelope means, since it specifically said, 'Pay up or suffer.' But that's not our main concern. If this guy got caught with his pants down, literally, the only way it would hook into killing Janice is if she was the blackmailer. I can't see that."

"I can't either. Janice never struck me as the greedy type." He ran his fingers through his already mussed hair and looked a little more adorable than usual. Put together Ben was nice. But Ben slightly disheveled was a whole other sexy animal.

And this line of thinking was definitely not helping our investigation. Plus, sexy or not, those pictures put me off from getting naked with even a slightly disheveled Ben. No way did I want to go to bed with someone who had spent the last ten minutes staring at that blonde's perfect, little, cellulite-less body. If he thought he was getting on to mine after that, which was seriously a far distance from perfect, little, or cellulite-less for that matter, he was so wrong. Sigh.

Ben had the envelope resealed and ready to take back to the bed and breakfast before dawn came. I looked at the clock on his mantel of pictures and winced at the time. "It's after midnight. I should probably go; I have to work tomorrow. Well, today, actually." I stood up from the surprisingly comfortable and yet still ugly-as-sin couch, and went to the piecrust table to pick up my keys from the wooden bowl. "You're going to take those back tonight, right?"

"Yeah, I'll get them back in, and we'll wait to hear what the police have to say tomorrow before officially crossing this guy off our list. Pictures or no pictures, there is still something wrong about the way he keeps demanding files that aren't his. But I did tell Dennis down at the station to look into the guy's alibi and whereabouts for the last week or so. Hopefully, Dennis will want to share with yours truly what information he finds, when he gets done, since I put him on the lead."

"Well, let me know what you find out, if anything. I feel like so much time has passed since her death and we're not getting anywhere. It's frustrating."

"I feel the same way, Ivy. We're going to have to be a little patient and let the police do their thing while we do ours."

This time there was no lascivious look in his eyes and I knew he was being totally sincere. I thought about the fact that Ben had a whole year to get to know Janice and see her around town. He had a lot more invested in this than I did. After all, I knew her only one evening.

"You're right, I'm sorry." I grabbed my discarded windbreaker and put it on in anticipation of the cold night air outside.

Ben stood from his position on the comfy-looking chair and walked over to me. The way he moved reminded me of a cat on the hunt. Stealthy and sleek, animal in his grace. Okay, now I was getting a little hokey and a lot turned on. Again.

Think of the blonde, think of the blonde, I reminded myself, and the urge to throw Ben on the convenient floor he'd mentioned earlier subsided a little. But before I could blink, he was next to me and his hands were tangled in my hair. His mouth swooped down on mine and I felt branded, owned, possessed. Those soft lips caressed mine as he massaged my scalp and made a low growl in his throat.

I thought I purred myself and wondered what kind of wild animal jungle sex I was missing tonight by going home to my cold, lonely bed. But Ben had things to do tonight, the least of which was to put the blackmail envelope back in Mr. Hedlund's room before the man came back from his hopefully very unpleasant night in jail.

Ben licked the seam of my lips and all other thoughts fled.

After we both came up for air, I walked my shaky legs out to my Santa Fe and Ben stayed in the open doorway until I had started the car and driven off. I watched him in my rearview mirror until I almost couldn't see him anymore and realized I was no longer on the pavement part of the road.

Back at the old homestead, and still shaky from my near collision experience with the drainage ditch on the side of the road, I wrapped up in a terrycloth robe and made myself some hot chocolate to chase away the cold.

I hoped Ben was safely back at his house and kicked myself for not asking him to call when he finished returning the goods. Even though Hedlund may not have been responsible for Janice's death, it didn't mean he wasn't culpable for something.

Looking at the clock, I realized it was after one a.m. and I'd better get into bed if I wanted to retain even half of my normal capacity for dealing with customers. I downed the hot chocolate and trundled myself off to that lonely, cold bed I'd thought of earlier and tried to snuggle down under the warmth of the covers.

Weird dreams of knights in tarnished armor and flappers dancing with caped men intruded into the few hours of sleep I got. So I was not a happy camper the next morning when Mr. Jorgensen and his wife came in about the cape with the dried blood, but I still tried to be nice. They were customers, after all, and even if he was innocent until I could prove him guilty (now that I'd essentially lost my prime suspect), she could still be a client, living the high life, while he was behind bars.

"Good morning, Mr. and Mrs. Jorgensen. How are you today?"

Perhaps I didn't pull the polite thing off very well, because she squinted her little eyes at him and he gave me a very odd look before answering. "We're fine, Ivy. Thanks for asking. I, uh, wanted to come in this morning because of the cape I dropped off last week."

Ah-ha! So he was going to try to get the cape back. He'd realized what incriminating evidence it had on it and now he needed to take it for a cleaning before he brought it back. Guilty, guilty man. My inner voice shook its head at the duplicity of people.

Mr. Jorgensen cleared his throat and I waited for the words to come out of his mouth. Words that would condemn him for the bad person he was. I was just sorry it had to be done in front of his wife.

"I, ah, wanted to see if the cape ended up with some blood on it and, if it did, say I was sorry. I thought I turned it in clean, until Doris went to wash my good white shirt I wore that night and saw the blood on it. I'd had a bloody nose before all the commotion— allergies—and thought I'd caught it all with the tissue, and kept it off your cape. But Doris showed me the stain, so I came down here to apologize, if necessary, and pay you that extra fee you charge for damaged articles."

A likely story, but then when I thought about it, it actually was a likely story. Why would this guy offer to pay for the cleaning fee and not even try to deny the blood? If I were a murderer I would try to get it back, then clean it myself or something. Besides, wouldn't Doris have questioned the stain?

"He has medicine to take for them darned allergies, but he never will. Too much of a guy, I guess," Doris said, seeming to pull the thought right out of my head. What was it with the people in this town and mind reading? "Anyway, we're real sorry about the whole thing, and I'm ashamed I didn't see it before we brought the costume in. I have this laundry potion, would have taken the whole thing out. Could have shared it with you instead of you having to send the cape out to the dry cleaners. I feel awful."

The woman was concerned about the dry cleaning bill and wanted to share a potion with me? Ah, small towns, gotta love 'em. Right?

Just then the phone rang, and since I'd told Kitty to take the day off, I was the only one here. "If the two of you will excuse me for a quick moment, I'll be right back and we can settle your account. Thanks for coming in, and I appreciate your time. I'll be right back."

I dove for the ringing phone, my head whirling with questions. I'd fumbled two suspects in a twenty-four-hour period. Or had I? Couldn't Doris be covering up for her husband? Or maybe she had fallen for the bloody-nose thing. Either way, I'd still wait to hear back from the police before I totally crossed him off my list, too.

I pushed the On button for the phone and was rewarded with a squawk and a woman's voice saying, "Please hold for the next available officer," which I took for a serious command to go find a spot where no one could hear me as I explained my idiocy. Oooo-kay. I ducked into the room between the main shop and the boudoir and hoped no one would come in.

Thirty seconds later, the deep voice of Detective Jameson came on the line. "Ms. Morris, is that you?"

"Yes, sir, it's me. And in fact, I have the customer we spoke about last week waiting in my front room. Is this about the cloak? Should I detain him?" Oh, God, had I jumped to conclusions and this call was because they'd caught Ben sneaking out of the cabin? Had he ratted me out and said I was there, too? Or had they found my fingerprints and were making sure I was here? That way when they came and arrested me, they didn't have to look for me?

All of a sudden I was very nervous as the detective cleared his throat. "Ma'am, you're not going to want to detain anyone. That would be our job." Oh, I was right, they were coming to get me. "The blood on the cape was from the wearer. We're assuming he nicked himself shaving or had a nosebleed or something. The hospital checked the blood against his donor card."

I guessed they weren't coming to cart me off to jail after all. "Detective, I appreciate the call and need to tell you the man just came in this morning to tell me it was a bloody nose that left the stain. I'm sorry for the trouble you went through." I really didn't want to lose a client over my active imagination. "Uh, is that okay instead of you talking to him? I really don't want to come across as some tale-teller, and since nothing was what I thought, I'd rather not lose a customer over it." Silence greeted me from the other end of the telephone. So I added, "Please."

A brief conversation was held on the other side of the phone line before the detective came back on. "All right, little lady." Perhaps he didn't remember meeting me. "That's fine for this time, but maybe next time you'll want to keep your nose out of things like this. Or ask your customers questions about stains before running to the police. Have a good day."

Then he hung up and I sat on the brocade couch, dazed. What the hell kind of police force did we have here if they didn't want to hear about possible leads from the average citizen? And had I just been totally dismissed as a feather-brained "little lady" because I brought something to them that didn't pan out? Well, now I was really going to find out who did this to Janice before they did. I'd show them "little lady."

I went back out to the main counter and dealt with Mr. and Mrs. Jorgensen. They went home happy and my register was a little bit fuller.

I wanted to check on Ben this morning and make sure everything had turned out okay. We also needed to put our heads together and come up with another suspect. I dialed the number Ben had given me and waited for him to pick up before I could breathe a real sigh of relief. Now for a new suspect. Yep, two suspects down. Who else could I wrongfully accuse?

Chapter Twenty-One

The sigh I'd been holding in came out as a whoosh when Ben finally answered on the fifth ring. After his "Hello," the only thing I could say was, "What the hell took you so long to answer? Jeez, I nearly ran over to the jail to see if you were there sharing space with that client guy."

He had the gall to laugh.

"I wouldn't have visited you, either," I said, snippy now.

"Oh, sweetheart. You wouldn't even have come for my conjugal visits?" His voice transmitted a huge smile, and I wished he were here right now so I could kick his perfect ass.

"You know, a little less cocky would look great on you." Obviously I was getting more comfortable with this whole new flirty, sharp side of myself. I didn't even blanch when the words came out of my mouth.

"You wouldn't want me to give up any of my 'cocky,' " he said in a sly voice that made me realize how that could have been, and obviously was, interpreted. Great. Thank God he wasn't here to see the cursed blush. So much for trying to match wits with Ben the Fallen.

"Yeah, yeah," I said, to cover up my embarrassment, and then went on to tell him about the call from the police and that we'd lost another suspect.

And Ben had news of his own. "Dennis, the policeman I was telling you about, called me just now. In fact that's who I was getting off the phone with when you called. He said Hedlund has a rock-solid alibi with his wife, who, by the way, is a tall, round, brunette. They were at a Harvest Party of their own and about a hundred people can vouch for seeing him throughout the evening, all the way to midnight. So he's not our guy either. And here's a new twist to the whole convoluted thing. I know you saw the stab wound on Janice, but it turns out from toxicology reports she was also poisoned. Any idea what to do next?"

I didn't have anything, but my plumber came in at that moment and I told Ben I'd have to call him back. "Hey, Charlie. In to finish up my fountain? It looks fabulous. I really appreciate you fitting this in." The fountain I'd ordered for the shop a little over a week ago was nearly done, and I was ecstatic.

"Yep, I should have this done tomorrow at the latest. Is everything looking good so far? No problems with customers or anything?"

"Actually everything is going great." I plastered a smile on and tried not to think about the fact that a lingerie thief and a murderer were still in our midst.

"Good. It looks like things are slow right now for you, so if you don't mind, I'll be working on the water line today. Ignore me and I'll get to work."

"Sounds good. I'll be in the storeroom if you need me." It was time to take another inventory of the remaining lingerie. I had replenished the plus-sized stuff, but business back there had been good lately, and it looked like I should order more of everything again.

Once inside the storeroom, I took a stool and sat

myself down, intent on doing my least favorite part of this new business. As I looked over what I had and marked down what to order, my thoughts were on Janice, stabbed and poisoned. Who needed to be that thorough? I didn't know, and all my leads were false so far.

Twenty minutes later, I was thirsty. I went into the front room to offer Charlie something from the fridge while I was there. He was leaning over the oval shape of the basin of the wall fountain. I opened my mouth to see if he wanted a soda out of the back when I realized he was showing the classic plumber's crack, and that crack was only slightly covered by pink lace. Oh. My. Word.

Pink lace. Pink lace? Why was there pink lace covering Charlie's plumber's crack? And what else, other than women's underwear, was made of pink lace and used under jeans? As soon as the thought ran through my mind, another stumbled along on its heels. Pink lace, women's underwear, women's lingerie, my missing women's lingerie. Oh. My. Word.

After all my wondering and speculating, could my underwear thief have been under my nose and in my shop, taking my money in a paycheck for his plumbing skills, while *wearing* my missing lingerie?

It was certainly a possibility. A possibility that made me sick to my stomach and pissed me off something terrible. But I'd already falsely accused two people of murder, so I wanted to be very careful this time. I tried to be nonchalant as I walked over by the newly installed fountain. The lingerie we carried had a distinctive tag and from experience I knew the tag could be seen at the top in the back of the panties. I made appreciative noises and tried hard to keep my face impassive as I told Charlie I was looking at his handiwork, instead of his butt crack.

Inside I was boiling like a blocked volcano. How dare he? Was he also wearing a bra? I looked at his snug T-shirt and saw no telltale signs of straps. Maybe he wore the bras at night at home. *Ew!*

He was about the right size for women's plus sizes. I'd estimate him at about a size sixteen, like his girlfriend, Jackie, my problem customer who wanted to wear a size two teddy. Maybe he was giving her the bras and keeping the underwear for himself. *Ew!* Again.

In fact, an episode with Jackie sprang to mind from last week. She'd come strolling into The Masked Shoppe and was showing off her new bra to Kitty. And Kitty, who happened to be Charlie's mom, was oohing and ahhing about the cut and style.

It seemed weird to me at the time because the only other place who sold bras big enough for Jackie was the discount thrift store around the corner. I was damn sure she wouldn't be caught dead shopping there, so my theory was making more sense.

I walked behind Charlie and tried to get a better look for the elusive tag but couldn't. Especially when he stood to show me some of the finer points of the way the fountain worked. The whole time he looked me right in the eye and smiled at my comments, chatting easily with me. Maybe I was wrong. I knew one way I could possibly find out. A quick phone call to Ben and my plan was in action.

Breaking and entering—Take Two.

But not so much breaking was going to be done, because the lights were ablaze in the house. Ben and I met around the corner from Charlie's house, where he actually still lived with his mom. So I guess that made it Kitty's house, but that wasn't making it any easier for me to think about breaking in.

I'd moved into Ben's vehicle after we saw all the lights in the house, and now we were playing the waiting game. "So, how was your day?" I said to break the silence.

"Good, and yours?"

I was about to answer when I realized he sounded distracted. I looked over toward the house and saw Charlie come out with the garbage cans. He looked like he was trying to move stealthily but wasn't quite pulling it off. He kept nervously turning his head left and right and was kind of up on his tiptoes. He looked funny, but there was nothing funny about this situation.

After depositing the cans on the edge of the curb, he raced back into the house, and we heard the door slam.

"I think it's too risky to go up and look in his trash right now," Ben said, turning toward me. "What about you, partner?"

I felt a warm glow. We were partners, and I thought he'd finally accepted me as part of this motley team now that I'd proven myself by doing my little bit of sneaky recon this afternoon.

"Sounds good. You want to grab some coffee and come back later, after all the lights are out? Hopefully that will mean Charlie and Kitty are in their beds. Maybe we'll only have to go as far as the trash to get our evidence. I really don't want to come back and try another time, and there is no way I'm breaking into Kitty's house while she's there."

Ben agreed, and we went to sit at Mad Martha's Milk and Munchies to have a cup of coffee and a piece of pie while we wasted some time. Mad Martha greeted Ben by name and gave me the eye, sizing me up. To make sure I was worthy of sitting with the town's sexpot, or trying to figure out why I would want to be seen with the infamous fallen one? I didn't know, but I wanted to eat in relative quiet. If she was sizing me up now, she would be doing it even more if we were still sitting here an hour from now. I decided to be proactive.

"Hi, Martha." I read her nametag to be sure it was actually Martha. Wouldn't want to make that mistake when I already had half the town giving me the evil eye. "How are you this evening?"

She seemed a little taken aback, so I pushed my advantage. "Ben promised me the best pie in town and told me we had to come here for it. I was wondering what you would recommend?"

And didn't Martha go all dainty and friendly on me. "Well, of course, honey. I bet you'd love a slice of my lemon meringue pie. It is divine. Why don't you and Ben have a seat, and I'll be right over. Would you like some coffee with that?"

"Of course. I heard Detective Jameson talking about the great coffee here, too. I'm sorry I haven't had a chance to come over and taste it for myself."

"Now, you don't worry about that. I know you're a busy woman. You can actually phone in an order to me in the morning and I could have my nephew run the whole thing over to you, you know."

"No I didn't know, but I will definitely keep it in mind. Thank you, Martha." I took the seat across from

Ben, in a booth he'd already picked out, and smiled sweetly at him.

"Pouring it on a little thick, don't you think?"

"Absolutely not, Mr. Fallon. It's all about customer relations and making nice with the people who might come in your shop."

"That's crap, and you know it." The dimple winked at me, and the mischievous smile sent my heart racing.

"All right, it's crap, but I didn't want her staring at me all night and possibly spitting on my pie, so I decided to be proactive."

"Smart move. It looks like we're even getting the big slice of the pie, too. Good job."

We smiled at Martha as she put our pie (which was huge) on the table and gave us two forks. "Good eating, kids. And Ivy, I'll be in this week to see about some stuff I've been meaning to try on."

She walked away, and I gave Ben a smug smile. "See?"

By ten o'clock we were back at Kitty's and ready to take on the world, or at least the trash cans. We parked in the spot around the corner again and walked the short distance to the curb where the cans stood.

"Now, you're sure Kitty doesn't have a dog?"

"I'm positive," I said as I walked on the uneven curb and tried to keep myself shielded by the big bushes separating the house from the street.

Ben was creeping behind me and I turned my head to speak to him. A scrambling noise made me whip my head back around to the front in time to see what I thought was a raccoon, except I couldn't really see his mask because of the bright neon green panties on his head.

One of the cans had tipped over and a big black trash bag was ripped down the side, spilling its contents across the pavement. And there, right there, was my proof, against Charlie at least. A rainbow of silk and lace cascaded out of the bag, and I bent to scoop everything back inside the black plastic.

Ben picked up a particularly "fancy" pair of panties and raised that one eyebrow before I snatched them out of his big hand and shoved them into the bag. Not wanting to make any noise, I didn't yell at him until we were a couple of blocks from the scene of the crime. I was thanking God we didn't actually have to go into the house, so my yelling was more for show than anything else.

"You are a miscreant."

"Am not."

"Are too."

"No."

"Yes. And I can't believe you were out there fondling women's underwear when I was trying to gather all the evidence."

"Yeah, well, I couldn't help myself. Crotchless panties are such a turn on."

"You are such a...such a *man*." And that said it all for me. He was such a man, but in a lanky, beautiful kind of way. It could possibly be I'd just decided to make him *my* man.

We drove back to his apartment, and since I'd promised him an explanation for why we had to go out to Kitty's house to do a little snooping, I prepared myself for a lecture on trying to do things on my own without him. He didn't disappoint.

"Of all the idiotic shit you have done and come up

with, this tops it. Why didn't you come to me when the stuff was first stolen? I would have helped you."

I paced the small confines of his living room, avoiding hitting the plush chair and the couch by not pacing in a straight line but more of a maze-like curvy meandering. "I wanted to handle it on my own."

"Then why did you call me in at the last moment?" I opened my mouth, but he didn't give me a chance to rationalize before he barreled on. "You could have come to me at any point and I would have helped, or at least been able to try to help you figure out what to do."

"Look, don't pull this macho crap with me. I wanted to handle things on my own and thought I was doing a good job, even if I wasn't getting anywhere. When we met up at the cabin, I thought about telling you, but then I knew how determined you were to figure out Janice's murder, and I didn't want to burden you with anything else."

"Well, you still could have told me." Something in those green eyes was different as he shifted his gaze from mine.

It was then I realized this wasn't just the testosterone talking, or a need to be included in everything. He really cared about me.

But where did that leave me? I'd been a tangle of emotions and needs since he'd first come up and whispered in my ear in the bar. But had everything been leading to this moment when his guard seemed to be down and he was sincere instead of his usual arrogant, confident self? Was this the side of Ben I'd felt had been missing and so had kept myself from really falling for him?

Of course the not-falling-for-him part was a crock,

because I had a sneaking suspicion much of the falling had been accomplished the night he came to the house and I thought he was an intruder. He'd stayed the whole night on my floor and never once tried to sweet talk me or force his way into my bed. Had I found what I'd been looking for all along? A sign I wasn't merely going to be some notch on his bedpost? My heart started beating so fast I thought I might be having a heart attack. And it certainly didn't slow down any when Ben started walking toward me in that sleek way he had.

I was a goner. He put his lips over mine and kissed me senseless. His hands cradled my face as he took his sweet time exploring each part of my mouth. It was swoon worthy. The taste of him exploded in my brain as his hand squeezed my tush for a brief second, then moved in a steady path straight up to my breast. After that it was all about feeling and enjoying the thrill I knew those big hands would be able to give me.

Chapter Twenty-Two

We were hot and heavy, roaming hands and panting breaths, when the shrill ring of the phone cut through a particularly yummy growl from the vicinity of my left thigh.

"Should you get that?" I asked, wanting to kick myself in the head. Hello? Why would I want him to do anything that was guaranteed to stop the delicious wanderings of his hands and tongue?

"No. No," he breathed against my flesh. He was getting closer to the place I most wanted him to be when the answering machine picked up.

"Ben, this is Marty." Ben's hands froze an inch from my skin, and I shuddered, groaning, and not in a good way. "I need you in here right now. Peter's out on a story, and I got a call about a burglary in progress that went all wrong. If you want me to take you seriously with this private investigator license thing, you'll get your ass down here as soon as you get this message." And then there was a click, and we both sat trying to get air back into our lungs.

Ben dropped his head onto my naked hip and I could feel his breath fan near my belly button. "My boss," he said.

Despite the lust and need clouding my brain, I could think well enough to realize this could be Ben's big break into crime reporting. The paper hadn't given him anything but his usual food critic stuff since he'd graduated from his online course, and he was getting down about the fact that he wasn't going anywhere. Now this opportunity fell into his lap just as I was about to get him in my lap. Sigh. I knew what I had to do. I tried to move out from under him, but his head was heavy on my hip and he gripped me tighter around the backs of my thighs.

"Don't move," he said, his voice low and strained. "Just don't move."

Um, okay. Could I at least talk? Apparently not before he did again.

"I can not believe this," he mumbled against my stomach. "I've waited and waited for them to notice me for this position and now, *now*, he calls."

"I was pretty impressed with your position." Good, Ivy, make a joke right now. That ought to get you another chance at seeing Ben's beautiful hair from an aerial view.

But he laughed and some of the tension seemed to drain from his body as his grip on my body loosened. "I don't want to go. I do not want to go right now."

And I don't want you to go, I thought. But I also didn't want to make this harder for him. "You have to go, Ben. This is your chance, and I don't want you to miss it." I combed my fingers through his hair and sighed. *Why is my life always like this?* I'd been an animal when we were in the thick of things, and now I felt like I'd stepped into one of those jaw traps you see on television.

Ben placed a kiss right on the swell of my hip that made my stomach jump. Then he got up in all his nude male glory and stalked across the room. "Do you hate me?" he turned and asked.

What? "What? Of course I don't hate you."

"I hate myself, that's why I asked. I want you, and here you are laid out like a dream." At least he didn't say turkey dinner. "A dream I crave, and I'm caught between wanting to ignore Marty to stay with you and running to the office. I'm an ass. Why did this have to happen now?"

"Ben, let me tell you, this is the way my life always works. I would have been surprised if nothing interrupted us. That's the way it is for me. I don't hate you, and you shouldn't hate yourself." I shifted on the couch—yes, the ugly couch, because we hadn't had time to make it to the bedroom—and pulled a pillow over my lap. "We'll have plenty of time to take up where we left off, but I don't want to be the one who kept you from taking the chance of a lifetime."

"You're being awfully understanding."

I was, wasn't I? Good for me. Then again, when I'd pulled the pillow over my legs it was because I could see them in the light spilling from the kitchen. Now that Ben wasn't between them, I didn't want him to get a good look without the benefit of heavy panting, which I assumed clouded the vision.

"I admit I wish you weren't leaving, but I also get why you have to. So go get dressed," I said, shooing him away with my free hand.

He seemed to struggle with himself for about a second before he sprinted down the short hallway, and I heard rummaging and muttering.

Jumping off the couch, I quickly retrieved my clothes from the floor, the lamp, and the corner of a large framed picture of a mountain range. Ben had some throwing arm.

By the time I was all put back together, except for my panties, which I could not find, Ben was hurtling back from the bedroom and ready to go.

"We'll pick up where we left off as soon as I get this story." He gave me a long, deep kiss that set my knees to jiggling and escorted me out to my car. "Thanks, Ivy, for understanding. I really appreciate it." And then he was gone and I was left standing in the parking lot, sans panties, on a frigid and windy night.

At home I crawled into my cold, lonely bed again and fell asleep after a lot of tossing and turning. The next morning I woke from a dream so hot I looked for burn marks on my sheets. Ben had been doing things to me I'd only heard of, and in return I was a sexually ferocious vixen. As I sorted through my closet looking for an outfit for today, I decided next time with Ben I'd try some of the dream moves, and that whipped-cream-and-ice thing I'd read about. I fervently hoped next time would be soon.

On the walk to work I planned my day and tried to find a time when I could call Bella and tell her about this new development in the life and times of Ivy. But apparently Bella had been using her non-existent psychic powers, because she was at The Masked Shoppe two minutes after I'd opened the door.

"So, Ivy, where were you last night?"

"Why?" But I knew my smug, self-satisfied smile gave me away.

"You little vixen. You and Ben? Down and dirty?"

"I was just calling myself the same thing. And yes, dirty with an extra R."

"No way."

"Yes way."

"No."

"Yes." Hadn't I had a similar conversation last night? And didn't that end up right where I hadn't thought I wanted to be? Which, of course, brought me back to hot thoughts of the wonderful things Ben and his hands, lips, and tongue had done to me. It almost sent my knees to jelly again.

"You have a twinkle in your eye."

"I don't doubt it."

"So I guess I don't have to ask how it was. Do I?" Bella fingered some of the costume jewelry hanging on a skeletal tree on the counter.

I laughed. "You can certainly ask, but I'm not going to tell you."

She looked at me, her face registering shock. "You won't tell me, your best friend in town?"

"My best friend, period," I said, laying my hand over hers and giving it a quick squeeze. "But no, I won't tell you. I didn't even tell my sisters when they each called this morning. It's like they have hormone ESP. Suffice it to say that what there was of it was incredible, and I will be doing it—and more—again, as soon as possible."

"You are bad." She took a necklace from the tree, gave it her attention, and then placed it back on its branch before looking at me again, a twinkle in her own eye. The twinkle flashed out after a second and she said, "Wait. What do you mean 'what there was of it'?"

So I had to explain about the infamous interruption. And after I talked Bella down from yelling at Ben about his priorities for the fifth time, she finally calmed down.

Thirty seconds later Kitty came in, putting a quick

end to our conversation by giving me the same look I'd seen over the past few days. It was a combination of confusion and some other emotions I couldn't quite put my finger on. She'd been distant and strange to me ever since the Harvest Ball, but I'd chalked it up to maybe some stress at home. Plus, I'd been so busy lately, and had so much on my plate with the shop, the theft, Janice's death, and trying to find her killer, I hadn't given Kitty and her petty nature a second thought. Only because Ben and I detoured into her neighborhood was I reminded of something she'd said on the Sunday after the dance. God, was that really only four days ago?

She'd been putting away stock and I came in to tell her we were moving the plastic swords to a different area for better traffic flow to the cash register. She kept her back to me and said, "It wasn't supposed to be like this when I ran the store."

Now, maybe I'd misinterpreted what she said, but since seeing Charlie in what was most likely my underwear, I'd begun to wonder about her. I also wondered what part she'd had, if any, in the lingerie going missing. I vowed to keep my eyes and ears open. Charlie would be in today, and his mother was already here.

Bella left after a little more whispered kibitzing. Two hours later, Charlie came lumbering into the store. I was in the storeroom and had a perfect line of vision to the fountain. Charlie bent over to place his tools on the side of the fountain, and I saw a glimpse of vibrant purple this time. Someone should really take the time to tell him not to bend over if he doesn't want the world to know his fetish, I thought.

Then I heard Kitty call for him, and I moved

quietly from the storeroom to the hallway outside my office. I guessed she'd decided to hold her impromptu meeting in my office without my permission. She really had been trying to take over lately, and I decided we might need to have a little talk about that sometime soon.

But my thoughts were cut off when Kitty's furious whisper reached my prying ears. "Why didn't you take anything last night? I told you to come in and take everything this time, not just the bras, and I saw everything is still here this morning. What is wrong with you?"

Ah-ha! So he had taken all the lingerie but only gave up the bras. I'd bet he gave the bras to Jackie; Kitty, with her little stick frame, would not fit in anything over a 32B.

"I'm done, Mom. I like Ivy, and I'm not going to mess things up for her again."

"You will if I say you will."

"No, I won't. Between you and Jackie, I'm about ready to take a long dive off a shallow cliff. So get off my back."

I heard a rustling sound and, afraid Kitty was about to come out, went back to the storeroom. Shoving aside several boxes, I grabbed my garbage bag of hidden evidence. I rushed back out because I wanted to corner them both at the same time and meet them head-on about their plans to "ruin me." But when I made it back to the office, only Charlie was standing there.

I had to make a quick decision. Did I want them together or should I divide and conquer? I didn't want to wait on this. It was too important. I still hated confrontation, but it was getting easier to do when people were threatening my shop and my livelihood—my reputation.

"Charlie, can I have a minute of your time?"

He jumped like I'd applied a cattle prod to his purple-silk-covered backside. "Uh, hi, Ivy. Uh, sure. I have a minute."

"Good," I said, as I pulled the trash bag from behind my back and dropped it on the floor in front of me. "Care to take that minute and explain this to me, then?"

His face blanched a truly pasty white, and his head dropped down. I waited impatiently for him to implicate himself and his mother, and maybe even Jackie, in this whole mess. In the meantime, my temper was really starting to boil. Images of me standing in the cold wind last night watching that raccoon walk away with my merchandise on his head made me hotter under the collar. How dare they?

Then Charlie started talking. "I'm really sorry, Ivy." Guilt and shame washed across his face, but there was a hint of something more. Something very close to calculation. "I took the lingerie, and I'm sorry. I know that's not enough. I can't return most of the stuff I took, but I did it alone and by myself. No help from anyone, and I made the decision solo. I wanted underwear, so I took underwear. Sorry. So, uh, are you going to call the police now?"

The look of careful calculation hadn't left his eyes yet, and it was now accompanied by an almost smile. Not a smarmy smile, like "ha-ha, I got you," more like "ah-ha, I've found a way out." I also noticed there was no mention of the mom-factor. He was totally taking the blame on himself, and I couldn't prove he hadn't acted alone; it would be my word against his. Should I leave Kitty out of it and deal with her on my own in another way?

"You want me to call the police?" I asked, then quickly backpedaled. "Of course, I'm going to call the police. Right now, as a matter of fact. You stay right there."

"I'm not going anywhere except to jail." He looked very satisfied with himself.

"I'm, uh, going to tie you to the chair until the police get here, okay?" That hadn't sounded very confident, but he sat down. I couldn't think of anything in the office I could use to tie him up, until my eyes fell on the bag of lingerie. I took out a pair of 3X peach elastic lace panties and made a big production of wrapping them around the arm of the office chair a couple of times before tying what I hoped was a good knot. Then I did the same thing with a pair of teal ones with no crotch. Ridiculous, I knew it, but without another idea, what was a girl to do?

I used the hi-tech three-line phone on my oak desk to place the call to the police department. We sat there, staring at each other as we waited for the cavalry. The whole time I wondered if I'd see Kitty again any time soon or if she'd stay away now that I'd gotten her son incarcerated.

"How bizarre," Bella said when I called to tell her what had happened. "I'm still a little peeved you didn't tell me about the missing lingerie before today, but I get that you wanted to do things on your own."

Bella understood because she had a family life similar to my own. She was the oldest and had successfully opened her own shop despite her parents' disapproval. I, on the other hand, had struck out on my own only because a shop had been given to me. There were some differences in how we got where we were, but the common thread was parental disapproval.

Speaking of my dad, he was due to fly into town in less than twenty-four hours. I told her I had to go and tried to remember if I had clean towels and sheets for his visit. I'd have to change the bed and fluff the comforter. I hoped this visit wasn't going to be awkward and that he wouldn't try to talk me back into the pink room.

He'd have a hard time convincing me to leave. I was now firmly ensconced in this little town, even if some of the residents still thought I was a freeloader. Besides, I was about to get laid by the hottest guy I'd ever seen.

Chapter Twenty-Three

I couldn't get hold of Ben until later that afternoon. I still needed to tell him about Charlie's arrest and my suspicions about Kitty.

His phone rang and rang. I was about to leave a sultry message that would knock his socks off and make him call back quickly, when he picked up. His gruff hello left me momentarily off-balance. I recovered and cleared my throat. "Hi, there."

"Hey, sexy lady."

I really hoped he couldn't hear my blush over the phone. "So I had a lot of excitement in the shop today, and I tried to get you on the phone but couldn't find you." That didn't sound like a nagging girlfriend, did it?

Apparently not enough to put him off. "Sorry about that. I was trying to track down some more information about Janice and who could have wanted to hurt her. I made some calls over to her hometown. I didn't find anything new by talking to her parents and people she knew, so I still have nothing."

He sounded so disappointed I started with my theory instead of the big arrest. "I think I have a way of figuring out who murdered Janice, but I need your help and Bella's. I was thinking we would meet and get a plan together. But in the meantime I have some excellent news."

"Does this have to do with the excitement in the shop?"

"Yes, it does, and wait till you hear how awesome we are at investigating."

"I'm all ears."

So I told him about overhearing Kitty and Charlie and about tying Charlie to the chair. By the time the police had shown up, Charlie was singing like a hound in the throes of passion about how it was all his plan and his fault. He took the blame for everything. When I tried to ask him about his mother's involvement, he vehemently denied that anyone else was in on the theft. I had a feeling he was happy to be getting away from a nagging mom and an angry girlfriend. He did say he had given the bras to Jackie, but as a gift, and she knew nothing about where they'd come from. Which made her stupid in my book, if she actually believed it. The police were not happy I had tried to solve the whole missing lingerie thing on my own, and they made sure to tell me never to do anything like that again.

But the best part was when they had to untie him from the chair and handle the crotchless panties. It was priceless. And that image would have to last me, because I was planning to go directly against their orders and play Columbo again with one last mystery before I gave it up to the police.

So we set the meeting for my house, tonight, with hopeful execution tomorrow before my dad came winging into town.

When I got home from the shop, feeling very proud of myself for figuring out the lingerie thing, I checked my messages because the red light on the phone was blinking. I put the speakerphone on and the voice from a few days ago, that one I couldn't originally tell if it was a man or a woman, came on the line with the force of a bullhorn.

"You have no idea what you're messing with, Ivy Morris. You need to go home and forget about this town. It should have been you, and I doubt Janice enjoyed falling in your place."

Despite thinking I knew who the voice belonged to and hopefully having a plan to get her, I was still scared. I called Ben, and, wouldn't you know, he ran right over. If I had any doubts about being in love with him, they all flew out the window when his car came to a rocking stop at my curb and he hustled up my front walk, determination clear on his face. My knight in tarnished armor.

"Are you okay?"

"Maybe you should listen to the message and tell me what you think," I said, leading him into the kitchen and replaying the message in all its glory on the speakerphone.

"Jeez, this person is not well. So now are you going to tell me who you think it is?" He took me into his strong arms and I rested my head on his collarbone. It made for a perfect fit.

"Let's wait for Bella."

Twenty minutes later, over dinner from the only restaurant in town that would deliver (my friends at Pizza Hut), Bella, Ben, and I went over my conclusions, thoughts, and feelings, throwing in observations of their own. We feasted on buffalo wings and cheese sticks as we went over all the equipment we needed and how best to play our hand. Basically, we hoped we knew what the hell we were doing and that we'd be able to catch our villain with a minimum of violence and bloodshed. Heaven help us, I thought, as I placed one call to my Great-Aunt Gertie's attorney and another to our intended victim.

Chapter Twenty-Four

The next morning dawned bright and early, with Ben having figured in more crazy dreams, some involving a swing and a shoe full of champagne. Bella had spent the night, leaving me no choice other than to remain celibate for a little while longer. Ben was adamant that our first time not include the stricture of Bella in the next room. He said he wanted me to feel free to scream.

He slept over, too, taking the foldout couch in my second bedroom, as Bella had already claimed my living room couch again. For some reason, he didn't want the floor and a boot pillow a second time. Go figure.

I walked out of my bedroom, following the smell of bacon and eggs into the kitchen. I found Ben there looking delicious, as always, and Bella wrapped in a huge robe the color of raspberries.

"Eggs," she said, placing a piled plate in front of me and grunting.

"Good morning to you, too," I said. I smiled at Ben across the table and felt his toes wander up the slit in my robe. My smile widened. While Bella fussed over another plate of food, I let my own foot trail up the inseam of his jeans and was very proud of myself for playing like this. I made what I hoped were sexy faces at him and watched as his dimples winked on. Point for me.

Sliding my foot higher up his leg, I scootched down in my chair a little to reach the bulge in his pants with my sock-covered toe. I gave him a naughty smile and a little giggle—really enjoying myself—when Bella stumbled from behind the stove, aiming for a chair at the table and rocking my chair in the process. My whole body lurched forward and Ben gave a great yell before bending over to grip his stomach, thereby smacking his head on the edge of the table in the process.

Needless to say, I was a little late when I showed up at the offices of Landon, Lerner, and Winnet. What with getting two bags of frozen peas for Ben and then leaving him in Bella's care when I realized what time it was, I streaked in the door halfway through the appointment.

Mr. Winnet welcomed me graciously, even though I was already a half-hour into my allotted time, and sat down with me. He offered me coffee and I declined, my stomach tied up into knots over what I was contemplating doing today.

"I appreciate your time, Mr. Winnet. I'm ashamed to admit I wasn't paying much attention when you read the official will after Gertie's funeral, and I have a few questions for you."

"Go ahead, Ivy. I was very fond of your great-aunt, and I'm willing to do whatever I can to help you."

So I told him as little as possible and asked the one question that would seal up my suspicions. "At this point, if I died, who would inherit The Masked Shoppe?"

His answer gave me the chills, but let me know I

was on the right track. I thanked him for his time and headed for the shop, where I had some serious preparing to do.

An hour later we were set, with Bella and Ben in their positions. The Masked Shoppe opened in an hour, but I had a very necessary appointment first.

There was a knock on the front door, and I wiped my sweaty palms against the sides of my skirt. If I had even one ounce of my sister the drama queen in myself, and if I had really grown a backbone during my time in my new town with my friends, this was the time to break it out.

I blew out a breath and walked to the door. "I will not be afraid. I have a plan, I have friends who will help me, and I have nothing to fear," I mumbled under my breath. Yes, I knew it was a little repetitive, but anything more difficult than that and I was afraid I'd start rocking myself in the corner.

I stared through the glass door before turning the brass knob, infusing my knees and my back with starch. I yanked the door open, smiling my best smile. "Kitty, I'm very glad you could come this early. Thanks for being punctual."

She seemed a bit unsure of herself until she crossed over the threshold into The Masked Shoppe. Then it was as if a switch were flipped. Her back straightened and her head came up. She was confident, assured, and ready to take the reins.

"Thank you for inviting me, Ivy. Now what was it that you needed to talk to me about?" She smoothed down the front of her melon-colored sweater set, then rested her hands on her gray slacks.

I offered her the cup of tea I'd made earlier and

watched as she let it sit there, not touching it because she was so intent on why I'd asked her to come to the shop. "Well, Kitty, I was hoping you and I could talk about the shop. I'm feeling a little overwhelmed here, and the bills don't pay themselves. I was thinking perhaps we could enter into some kind of agreement where you would own a part of the shop and we could be partners. I talked with Mr. Winnet this morning, and he told me how disappointed you were when Gertie left me the shop instead of you. And I know you must be distraught over Charlie's arrest. I thought maybe I could help you give your life some purpose by making you a manager. You would have some responsibility, and I'd give back your key. Of course, you wouldn't be a full partner, but maybe this way we could all get a little something we want." I paused, then offered to go get the paperwork I'd had the attorney draw up as a prop.

"Yes, I'd like to see what you have in mind. Thank you." Her voice made it sound like she wanted to add, "you bitch" on the end of that. She twitched a little in her seat, and I could almost see her brain replaying my words. Thinking about how little I was actually giving her, how she'd have to settle for a lot less than she'd wanted, and how her son was in jail for stealing my lingerie. By this time she must have known I knew she was in on that little scheme, too.

I was counting on her being desperate. When I went back into my office, I watched her on my newly installed security camera. Ben was nice enough to pull strings for me to get it last night. This setup meant I had a front row seat when she took a couple of capsules out of her purse and broke them into the cup sitting in front of my seat in the main room.

I timed my re-entrance so I could sit down with the paperwork before she had time to take a sip of her tea. "If you'd like to read over them now, that would be fine," I said as I lifted up my teacup. I saw the anticipation, the sick glee in her eyes as I brought the cup to my lips.

Then I pretended to sniff it and pulled it away from my nose quickly. The light dimmed in her eyes and then died as I said, "Oh, Kitty, I'm so sorry. I placed the wrong cup in front of you. This is the chamomile I made for you and I had the Earl Grey. I apologize. Silly me, I almost had you drinking sugar, and we both know how your system can only handle Sweet-N-Low." I'd remembered that little tidbit from Bella, who used to do Kitty's hair and got yelled at if Bella made Kitty's tea wrong.

I saw the way her eyes widened and the very earth seemed to stop when her brow crinkled. I almost heard her snap. Then she was a whirl of activity as she jumped up and threw the table at me, making a mad dash for the door. Or so I thought, until she turned back with one of the rapiers we carried and started advancing toward me with malice in her eye.

"You ruined everything," she said, breathing heavy and rasping her words. "You ruined everything for me, and now I'm going to pay you back."

"Now, Kitty..."

"Don't you 'Now, Kitty' me, you oversized cow. I had the perfect plan, and you were supposed to hightail it out of here when your store was burglarized. You, being a coward and all, were supposed to get all girly on me and go back to your Southern California and your sun and your year-round tan. But no, you had to snoop around instead of taking my barbs to heart and the lingerie as a warning against bad things happening."

Was this the part where I was supposed to keep her talking? Because I was getting creeped out and thinking I ought to either get the hell out of here or grab up my own rapier. But Kitty blocked both the front door and the wall with my brand new, really nice display of plastic swords.

"Then you didn't even have the decency to die at that Barn party. You made me kill an innocent woman I really liked. Janice was nice, whereas you are the spawn of Satan."

"I made you kill Janice? You poisoned Janice and the only thing you have to say for yourself is that it's someone else's fault?" Okay, not doing so good on keeping her talking and not making her angrier. Now she started advancing on me with her little plastic sword. The rapier might have been made of plastic, but it was hard plastic. Those babies could sting if slashed through the air.

"Yes, you horrendous bitch. *You* made me kill Janice. You were the one in the flapper costume, and you told me yourself you were wearing the blue mask. I saw you with the wig on the counter. You were supposed to be dressed like Janice was, and I brought you a glass of champagne with the poison. I watched you down it in one gulp. Except it wasn't you, and so it's your fault she's dead. You were supposed to faint and then wake up scared, and bolt for home like the frightened heifer you are. But I gave her too much of the stuff. Your fat ass would have just fainted, but it was too much for Janice. I saw her eyes roll back and she dropped dead away. But then I had to be sure, because she'd seen me right before I realized she wasn't you." She advanced on me again, nostrils flaring. "So I had to stab her with a pair of scissors from my purse. And now it's your turn to die. You put my son in jail and took my store, and now you'll die in it."

Her logic was obviously askew. How did she think she would get the store, or even get away, for that matter, once she killed me? And she was about to pay dearly for her cow and fat references. Besides, even if she managed to put the hurt on me, I had my backup in place.

"Kitty, what do you think you're going to do with that sword?" I said this, cool as a cucumber, and waited for her reply. Instead I felt a distinct stinging on my bare forearm. "You hit me!"

"You're damn right I did, and there's a lot more where that came from." She grabbed a silk belly dancer scarf off the same wall and tried to wrap it around my wrist. All the while she was mumbling things about Charlie skulking around my house on the night of the Ball and using a similar scarf to muffle her voice during her threatening phone calls. She snapped the sword at me again.

Before I could blink, she'd wrapped the scarf around me from elbow to wrist, and a sneer popped out on her face. I had to give her points for swiftness. "You are done. I have more of the poison in my bag, and you'll be gone before you can say, 'The Masked Shoppe.'"

I tried to wriggle out of her clutches, but she was seriously stronger than her little body looked. She tied my arm to a spindle chair and walked over to where she'd placed her purse on the sales counter. At that precise moment, the cavalry burst in. The portly Detective Jameson and his trusty sidekick, the perfectly coiffed Detective Bartley, were followed closely by Ben and Bella.

Chapter Twenty-Five

Still holding the discarded rapier at my side, I watched Detectives Jameson and Bartley cuff a screaming Kitty and shove her into the back of their unmarked car. With a deep satisfaction and a feeling of having finally won, I turned to Ben and Bella and smiled at them.

"Glad that's over," I said, wiping my sweating forehead with the scarf dangling from my arm.

Ben swept me up in a huge hug and kissed me so hard I thought my toes not only curled up but would fall off. When the kiss ended and my head stopped revolving like a disco ball at a high school dance, he whispered in my ear, "We are definitely finishing what we started. Tonight." Then he let me go long enough for Bella to hug me to her.

"You were so brave," Bella said, releasing me. She hit me in the arm. "Don't ever scare me like that again. Who was the one who said Kitty would go docilely once you told her the jig was up? Who said it would be a piece of cake? You. And I, for one, will never believe you again about stuff like that. She could have killed you!" This was punctuated by another jab to the arm Kitty had smacked with her plastic sword.

"Watch it," I said and rubbed my arm where Bella had managed to hit me twice in the same spot. "I'm sorry, okay? I thought she would give up once she figured out we knew everything. I mean, I wanted her desperate, but I still thought she'd retain some smarts. I guess I was wrong."

The car holding the detectives and Kitty slowly pulled away from the curb. Several spectators came out to see what the commotion was all about. She raised her cuffed hands and very deliberately gave me the finger through the back window. I told all the gawking people to look for Ben's byline tomorrow in the *Martha Herald*, which reminded me. "How was your first assignment?" I asked him.

"Uh, all right. I don't really want to talk about it right now."

"What do mean you don't want to talk about it?" Bella asked, and I gave him my version of the bewildered look on her face.

"Well, it, um, wasn't quite what I thought." He pulled at the collar of his T-shirt and looked distinctly uncomfortable.

"Spill," I said. "What was it, then?"

"Remember that story I told you about the man trying to find the owner of that stray dog?"

Bella and I looked at each other, remembering the story of the guy who came in to fill out an advertisement for a lost dog. The poor animal's only defining characteristics were sticking his nose in any female crotch and humping hedges. We both snickered and looked back at Ben. "Yes," we said in unison.

"Well I guess Rudder, which is what the old guy decided to name the dog when nobody came to claim the stupid thing, trapped the next door neighbor's poodle behind a shed and got on her. When the neighbor heard her dog's shrill barking, she went out and found them. She ran next door and grabbed this guy and was screaming about pedigree and stuff, demanding he get his mangy dog off her purebred. They tried everything, but the humper was not letting go. They finally had to call a veterinarian to get them to separate, and Marty put me on the story because he wanted to make sure I was committed to being a part of the team. Nice intro, huh? Not quite a burglary in progress. More like a humping gone wrong."

About halfway through the story I started snorting with laughter. Even after he was done telling it I still couldn't stop myself. Cocky, self-confident Ben Fallon, doing a story on perpetually humping dogs. Life was rich.

That evening, Ben came over as I was finishing up cleaning my home for my dad's arrival. Dad never had called to tell me how long he was staying, so somehow I had to tell Ben that sex was going to be a difficult thing to do as long as my dad was here.

I knew Ben was disappointed, but I did tell him maybe we could figure something out between us. Then he got right into the reason he'd stopped by, other than to see the lovely yours truly.

"I was down at the station trying to get facts for my story about Kitty and her arrest. While I was there, I picked up two very good pieces of information."

"Yeah, what's that?" I asked as I grabbed him around his waist and snuggled under his chin in "my place."

"Well, first of all, Kitty is in a shitload of trouble. She'll get time for killing Janice and the attempt on your life. But she's also going to get time for forging a doctor's signature to get the prescription she used to poison Janice and dropped in your cup to get you."

"Really?" I was laughing. "That is wonderful."

"I thought you'd also like to know that when she was put in her cell, she had a neighbor. You'll never guess who it was."

"Who?" Oh, I could think of many people I wouldn't mind Kitty being next to. How about Jeffrey Dahmer or Ted Bundy?

"Charlie."

"Oh, man, that guy cannot catch a break." I laughed again because it was too good. I really thought Charlie had given himself up in hopes of getting away from his mother, and now she was in the cell right next to his. He had to be screaming his head off.

"And..."

"There's more?"

"Yes, there's more." Ben put his chin on top of my head, and I could feel his jaw working as he said the rest of his great news. "Samuel Hedlund was being blackmailed by his own wife, if you can believe it. Pretty smart woman. She took those pictures and then mailed them from the next town over. She wanted to bleed him dry before she divorced him. So she attached the photos as a virus to every file in his hard drive and they would piggyback onto the files he sent or downloaded to disk, like the ones he gave to Janice for his annual reports."

I was impressed. "That *is* clever. I'll have to remember that one."

"You won't need it, Ivy. I may have had a wandering...eye." That's not what I would have called it, I thought. "But that's over now. I want you," he said, backing me up against the arm of the couch. "Every single creamy inch of you." I fell backward and he followed me down, his mouth fastening to the place right behind my ear that drove me mad. "This couch is comfy. Let's give it a try."

At that moment, with Ben kissing me into oblivion, the doorbell rang. I looked out the stained glass panels and could see the top of my dad's bald head as he looked down at something I couldn't see. Blasted bad timing, I thought.

Ben bent so his forehead rested on mine. "We'll pick up where we left off next time," he said.

Next time couldn't come soon enough.

A word about the author...

Misty Simon loves a good story and decided one day that she would try her hand at writing one. Eventually she got it right. There's nothing better in the world than making someone laugh, and she hopes everyone at least snickers in the right places when reading her books. She lives with her husband, daughter, and two insane dogs in Central Pennsylvania, where she is hard at work on her next novel or three.

She loves to hear from readers so drop her a line at:
misty@mistysimon.com
www.mistysimon.com

CPSIA information can be obtained
at www.ICGtesting.com
Printed in the USA
BVHW041557280921
617680BV00016B/591

9 781628 302356